The Fate of the Fallen

KEVIN SHAH

Chennai • Bangalore

CLEVER FOX PUBLISHING
Chennai, India

Published by CLEVER FOX PUBLISHING 2025
Copyright © Kevin Shah 2025

All Rights Reserved.
ISBN: 978-93-67070-52-9

This book has been published with all reasonable efforts taken to make the material error-free after the consent of the author. No part of this book shall be used, reproduced in any manner whatsoever without written permission from the author, except in the case of brief quotations embodied in critical articles and reviews.

The Author of this book is solely responsible and liable for its content including but not limited to the views, representations, descriptions, statements, information, opinions and references ["Content"]. The Content of this book shall not constitute or be construed or deemed to reflect the opinion or expression of the Publisher or Editor. Neither the Publisher nor Editor endorse or approve the Content of this book or guarantee the reliability, accuracy or completeness of the Content published herein and do not make any representations or warranties of any kind, express or implied, including but not limited to the implied warranties of merchantability, fitness for a particular purpose. The Publisher and Editor shall not be liable whatsoever for any errors, omissions, whether such errors or omissions result from negligence, accident, or any other cause or claims for loss or damages of any kind, including without limitation, indirect or consequential loss or damage arising out of use, inability to use, or about the reliability, accuracy or sufficiency of the information contained in this book.

CONTENTS

1. The Wizard of Elysia 1
2. The Hidden Blade 4
3. The Forest's Embrace 7
4. A Clash in the Shadowed Grove 11
5. Echoes of the Past 14
6. The Fallen King 19
7. The Fortress of Shadow and Light 23
8. Shadow and Fire 26
9. The Gathering Storm 30
10. The Dawn of Reckoning 35
11. The Dark Knight Rises 40
12. The Gift of Gratitude 43
13. The Dark Council 47
14. The Veil of Deception 51
15. The Last Stand 55
16. Breaking the Veil 59
17. Shadows of Destiny 62
18. The Rebirth of the King 65
19. Time for Reclamation 69
20. The Waging War 73
21. The Dual Reign 78
22. A Villain Made 82
23. The Call to Arms 86
24. Schemes of the Shadowed Siege 90
25. Prelude to Destruction 94
26. The Strategist's Gambit 98
27. The Battle Unfolds 102
28. The Battle Unfolds: Part II 106
29. The Madness of War 110
30. Wrath of the Fallen 115

Contents

31. The End of An Era: the New Proclamation 119
32. The Leader's Farewell 124
33. Between the Waves and Stars 128
34. A Bond Forged in Solitude 132
35. The Spark of Innovation 135
36. Blueprints of Hope 139
37. The Grand Fiesta 143
38. Faith and Facade 147
39. Shifting Shadows 151
40. Threads of Treachery 157
41. Beneath the Surface 161
42. Bonds Broken 166
43. The Hunt Begins 169
44. Into the Abyss 172
45. Bound By Bloodshed 174
46. Old Valour, New Vices 177
47. Tides of War 181
48. The Fire's Reach 185
49. The Shield of Sacrifice 188
50. The Loss of the Fallen 192

1

THE WIZARD OF ELYSIA

The twilight woods whispered secrets only those attuned to magic could hear. Valyron moved carefully through the dense undergrowth, his dark cloak blending with the shadows of the towering trees. His sharp eyes scanned the surroundings, every rustle of leaves and distant call of birds feeding his constant vigilance.

He wasn't here for peace, though the serenity of the place could easily fool a wanderer into forgetting their purpose. No, Valyron was here for something more elusive—more dangerous. His fingertips brushed the small medallion hidden beneath his robes, a relic that pulsed with an ancient energy. It had led him here, deep into the heart of the Elysian Wood, in search of a clue. A single feather, they said, could lead to the mythical Firebird.

But legends had a way of turning into obsessions.

Valyron paused by a fallen log, kneeling to inspect the strange markings etched into its bark. His mind raced, piecing together the runes and symbols, remnants of an ancient ritual long forgotten by most. To anyone else, they would mean nothing—simple scratches in the wood. But to Valyron, they spoke of fire, of life reborn from ashes, and of power that could shape kingdoms.

His gaze darkened. He'd sacrificed too much, come too far to let this trail grow cold. Yet, beneath his determination, doubt festered. What if he never found the Firebird? What if his entire quest, everything he had worked for, was built on nothing but myths and dreams?

As he stood up, his hand unconsciously tightened around his staff. The familiar hum of magic responded, the air around him shimmering with barely contained energy. A reminder that he wasn't just a seeker—he was powerful. But even power came with its own price.

Suddenly, a sharp sound cut through the stillness—a twig snapping, deliberate. Valyron's senses flared, and he spun around, his staff raised, magic ready to be unleashed. But the forest remained still, the shadows playing tricks with his vision. Whatever—or whoever—it was had disappeared into the woods just as quickly as they had come.

With a deep breath, Valyron lowered his staff. The Firebird's feather wouldn't wait for him. There was no time to waste on ghosts.

Meanwhile……

The streets of Virestone bustled with life as merchants hawked their wares and travellers from distant lands filled the narrow roads with tales of their journeys. But Leo wasn't here for stories. He was here for something much more practical—gold.

He slipped through the crowd with practiced ease, his movements fluid as he avoided jostling shoulders and watchful eyes. The weight of the pouch at his side was a comforting reminder of the day's work. A few bets won, a couple of deals struck, and one or two purses lifted from those too distracted by their own greed. All in a day's work.

But behind the confident smirk, Leo couldn't shake the feeling that he was running out of time. Sure, the thrill of the game kept him going, but there was more to it than that. There had to be.

The town square opened up before him, its centrepiece a grand fountain where children splashed and laughed, their carefree joy a stark contrast to the weight Leo carried on his shoulders. He approached the fountain, his reflection rippling in the water. What did he really want? To be the best swordsman? The richest rogue? None of it seemed to matter as much as it once did.

As he leaned on the stone edge, lost in thought, a sudden voice behind him brought him back to reality.

"Hey, you! Stop right there!"

Leo's instincts kicked in. Without thinking, he darted into the nearest alley, the shouts of the guards following close behind. His heart raced, but his feet knew the path well. This wasn't the first time he'd had to outrun trouble.

But as he turned a corner, something strange happened. The noise of the town faded, and the narrow alley seemed to stretch longer than it should have. The walls closed in, shadows deepening. Leo's steps faltered as the world around him seemed to blur and shift.

Before he knew it, he was no longer in Virestone. The cobbled streets gave way to soft earth, and towering trees replaced the stone buildings. The air was different here—thicker, more alive. Leo blinked, his breath catching as he realized he was no longer alone. He'd been led into something far bigger than a simple chase.

The forest around him was quiet, almost too quiet. And then, from the depths of the shadows, a figure emerged—tall, cloaked, with eyes that gleamed like embers in the dark. Leo's hand instinctively went to his sword, but something held him back.

This wasn't a threat. Not yet, at least.

The figure stepped forward, and in the fading light, Leo could make out the features of a man—no, not just a man. There was something otherworldly about him, a presence that demanded attention.

"You shouldn't be here," the figure said, his voice calm but carrying an undeniable weight of authority.

Leo raised an eyebrow, his grip on his sword loosening but not releasing. "Funny. I was about to say the same to you."

The man smiled faintly, though it didn't reach his eyes. "I'm Valyron. And you've stumbled into something much larger than yourself."

Leo's heart raced, but he kept his expression neutral. "Is that so? Well, Valyron, it seems like you and I have a lot to talk about."

The two stood there, in the quiet of the forest, both unaware that this meeting would change the course of their lives forever.

2

THE HIDDEN BLADE

*L*eo, clad in rugged travel attire, had stepped into the dense forest that lay at the edge of his wanderings. The canopy above was thick, filtering sunlight into a gentle, dappled glow. Each step he had taken on the leaf-strewn path felt deliberate, as if the forest was determined to make the two meet.

Valyron said, "Well, this jungle is not safe for a person who has no tools to keep him secure. Here, have this spare blade I have. You anyways look like you can handle a sword. However, if you want an upgrade, I have heard some legends about this place. The Alarician Blade! But only the worthy are able to get this sword. If you have it in you, I think you should venture into the forest to find it. I must go now." Valyron left Leo's side with some inspirational words that just changed Leo's intentions. His mind shifted from gambling and robbery to becoming a warrior.

His journey so far had been fraught with challenges, but none as daunting as the forest's unnerving silence. Every now and then, the distant sound of rustling leaves would break the stillness, leaving Leo on high alert. As he ventured deeper, a palpable sense of unease grew. He felt as if eyes were watching him, but he couldn't see anyone.

Suddenly, the ground beneath him trembled, and Leo's instincts kicked in. He dove to the side just as a colossal stone slab crashed down where he had been standing. Rising quickly, he faced the source of the disturbance: a formidable stone guardian emerged from the shadows, its massive form and glowing eyes radiating an ancient, magical energy.

The guardian's presence was commanding, a giant carved from stone and imbued with enchantments. It was clear that this was no ordinary sentinel; it had been conjured to protect the sword Leo sought.

The Hidden Blade

Without hesitation, Leo grabbed a sturdy branch from the ground and readied himself. The guardian's eyes glowed fiercely, and it swung its massive stone fists with surprising agility. Leo dodged the first attack, narrowly escaping the crushing blow. He knew brute strength alone would not win this battle; he needed strategy.

Leo's gaze swept over the battlefield. The forest floor was littered with ancient runes and symbols etched into the ground, partially obscured by dirt and debris. It dawned on him that these markings might be linked to the guardian's weaknesses.

As the guardian charged again, Leo rolled beneath its outstretched arm and slid across the ground to reach one of the runes. His fingers traced the intricate symbols, and a plan began to form. He recalled ancient tales of such runes being used to bind or weaken magical constructs.

The guardian was relentless, and its attacks grew more furious as it sensed Leo's strategy. Leo leapt from side to side, avoiding the guardian's blows while working to decipher the runes. With a deep breath, he activated a series of runes with a quick incantation, causing a shimmering barrier to form around the guardian.

The barrier emitted a soft glow and began to pulse, weakening the guardian's magical defences. The guardian roared in frustration as its movements slowed, revealing cracks in its stone form. Seizing the opportunity, Leo dashed forward, dodging the guardian's increasingly erratic attacks.

With a final, decisive strike, Leo used a sharp fragment of a broken rune as a makeshift weapon. He aimed for the cracks in the guardian's stone exterior, targeting its core. The guardian let out a thunderous cry as Leo's makeshift blade struck true, causing the stone to shatter and crumble into debris.

Breathing heavily, Leo surveyed the fallen guardian. It had been a fierce opponent, but Leo's ingenuity and quick thinking had turned the tide. He approached the place where the guardian had been stationed and discovered a hidden alcove.

Inside, resting upon a pedestal bathed in a faint, otherworldly light, was the legendary sword of Alaric. Its blade gleamed with an ethereal brilliance, reflecting the forest's filtered light. Leo approached it with a mixture of awe and determination.

As his hand closed around the hilt, he felt a surge of power coursing through him, a confirmation of his worthiness. The sword was both heavy and light, resonating with an energy that felt both ancient and familiar. Leo knew that this weapon was more than a mere tool; it was a symbol of his growth and the challenges he had overcome.

With the sword in hand, Leo exited the forest, his resolve stronger than ever. He had faced a formidable challenge and emerged victorious, proving his worthiness not just to the sword, but to himself. As he continued his journey, he felt a renewed sense of purpose, ready to face whatever lay ahead with newfound strength.

3

THE FOREST'S EMBRACE

Valyron stood at the edge of the ancient forest, the towering trees looming over him like silent sentinels. Their branches interwove high above, creating a dense canopy that filtered the sunlight into a soft, dappled glow. The forest's inviting yet enigmatic presence stirred a mix of apprehension and anticipation within him. Clutching the staff that had been his constant companion since he was fifteen, Valyron took a deep breath, letting the calming energy of the wood seep into his veins.

The staff, a cherished heirloom passed down from his parents, was not just a tool of his trade but a symbol of his heritage. Crafted from dark, polished oak and engraved with intricate runes, it was a potent artifact imbued with the magic of generations past. His father had presented it to him on his fifteenth birthday with solemn pride. "This staff is more than a weapon," he had said, his eyes glistening with both love and expectation. "It carries our family's legacy. Let it guide you, protect you, and make us proud."

Valyron's heart ached with the memory of his parents, now long deceased. He had ventured into the forest not just in search of adventure but with the hope of honouring their memory. The forest, with its ancient magic and untamed beauty, was a place where he hoped to prove himself worthy of the legacy entrusted to him.

The forest path twisted and turned, a labyrinth of nature's design. With each step, the forest seemed to come alive. The air was thick with the scent of pine and damp earth, while the occasional rustle of leaves hinted at unseen creatures moving through the underbrush. Valyron's senses were on high alert, his staff clutched tightly as he navigated the treacherous terrain.

His journey was marked by a series of trials that tested both his physical prowess and magical skill. The first trial came unexpectedly. As he rounded a bend, the ground beneath him shifted, revealing a large, hulking figure emerging from the shadows—a guardian of the forest with the body of a bear and the head of a serpent. Its scales shimmered with an iridescent sheen, and its eyes glowed with a menacing light.

Valyron's heart raced, but he quickly assessed the situation. The guardian's massive frame and powerful limbs made direct confrontation seem unwise. He knew he had to rely on his wit and the power of his staff. He took a deep breath, focusing his mind as he channelled the energy from the staff into a spell. The runes along the staff began to glow with a soft, golden light, illuminating the clearing and casting long shadows.

With a resolute voice, Valyron began chanting an incantation, weaving an intricate spell designed to calm and confuse the guardian. The words flowed from his lips with practiced ease, the magic resonating through the staff and the forest around him. The guardian hesitated, its aggressive stance faltering as the golden light enveloped it.

Valyron took advantage of the creature's disorientation. He swiftly conjured a series of illusions, creating multiple images of himself that seemed to flicker and dance around the guardian. The creature, now thoroughly confused, roared in frustration, its eyes darting from one illusion to another. The illusions made the guardian's task of finding and attacking the real Valyron nearly impossible.

With the guardian's focus diverted, Valyron drew upon the staff's power to cast a binding spell. He extended his hand, and the runes on the staff glowed brighter, forming a network of magical restraints that snared the guardian in shimmering, ethereal chains. The creature struggled against the bindings but was unable to break free.

Exhausted but triumphant, Valyron approached the subdued guardian. He whispered a few words of gratitude and respect, acknowledging the creature's role as a guardian of the forest. The magical restraints dissipated, and the guardian retreated into the shadows, leaving Valyron alone in the clearing. He wiped the sweat from his brow and looked at the staff with renewed respect. It had proven its worth, just as his father had promised.

As Valyron continued his journey deeper into the forest, he encountered other challenges. The forest was not merely a place of beauty but also a realm of trials. Ancient spirits of the forest posed riddles that tested his knowledge and wit. He solved each riddle with careful thought, his mind working in harmony with the magic of the staff.

The terrain itself was a challenge. Steep inclines and treacherous roots made each step a careful negotiation. Valyron's agility and balance were put to the test, and he used his staff as a walking stick and a tool to steady himself. The forest seemed to respond to his every move, its magic both aiding and hindering him.

One particularly difficult obstacle was a series of ancient symbols carved into the trunks of the trees. These symbols glowed faintly with an otherworldly light, and Valyron recognized them as part of a complex spell that required him to decipher their meaning. He used the staff to interact with the symbols, tracing their patterns in the air and invoking the ancient magic they represented. Each correct interpretation revealed a hidden path or unlocked a new area of the forest.

The deeper Valyron ventured, the more the forest seemed to pulse with ancient magic. The air grew thicker with enchantment, and the bioluminescent fungi that dotted the forest floor cast an eerie, otherworldly glow. The sense of anticipation grew stronger with each step, and Valyron could feel the weight of the forest's history pressing down on him.

After what felt like an eternity of trials and challenges, Valyron arrived at a secluded clearing. The clearing was bathed in the soft light of an ethereal glow, and at its centre stood a pedestal with an ornate box resting upon it. The staff's runes flared with intensity as if guiding him towards the box. He approached cautiously, the anticipation mounting with each step.

The box was exquisitely crafted, adorned with intricate designs and encrusted with gemstones that reflected the ambient light. Valyron reached out, his fingers trembling slightly as he touched the lid. With a reverent motion, he lifted the lid to reveal a crystal orb, pulsating with a soft, inner light. The orb seemed to resonate with the staff's magic, creating a harmonious aura that filled the clearing.

As he held the orb aloft, Valyron felt a surge of power and connection, as if the orb was a conduit to the very essence of the forest's magic. The orb's warmth spread through him, affirming that he had completed his quest and honoured his parents' legacy. The forest seemed to exhale in relief, and the magical energy surrounding him intensified.

Valyron stood in the clearing, the staff and the orb in hand, feeling a deep sense of accomplishment. The trials he had faced and the lessons he had learned were etched into his memory, and he knew that this journey had changed him. He made his way back through the forest, each step marked by a renewed sense of purpose.

As he emerged from the forest, Valyron looked back one last time. The ancient trees stood silent and majestic, their presence a reminder of the magic and legacy that had guided him. With the staff and the orb in hand, he was ready to face whatever challenges lay ahead, knowing that his parents' spirit and the forest's magic were with him.

4

A CLASH IN THE SHADOWED GROVE

As Valyron moved forward, he came across another forest. The forest hummed with an eerie stillness as the moon cast its silver glow through the thick canopy. Leo, still shaken from his unexpected encounter, was now wandering cautiously through the dense undergrowth. His heart raced, not from fear but from the chaotic mix of adrenaline and curiosity. Every rustle in the dark seemed amplified, as if nature itself was whispering secrets he could not quite grasp.

Suddenly, a sharp sound broke the silence—a crack like a twig snapping underfoot. Leo spun around, his eyes narrowing into the darkness. Before he could react, a figure emerged from the shadows, moving with the grace of a seasoned warrior. Leo's instinct was to draw his sword, but before he could, the figure was upon him.

Valyron, his staff glowing faintly in the moonlight, confronted Leo. The staff, a majestic piece of craftsmanship, was adorned with intricate carvings and a crystal orb at its tip, pulsating with a soft, ethereal light. The two adventurers stood face to face, tension crackling in the air.

"Who goes there?" Valyron demanded, his voice steady yet laced with authority.

Leo, taken aback, instinctively raised his sword. "I could ask you the same question. This is my territory."

Valyron's eyes flicked to Leo's weapon and then back to his face. "You! So, we meet again. Listen, I'm not here to fight you. I was on my way to the heart of the forest for my own reasons. But it seems our paths have crossed."

Leo lowered his sword slightly, still wary. "Don't worry, in fact I am sorry, I wasn't expecting to bump into anyone, let alone someone with a staff that glows like a beacon. What brings you here?"

Valyron's expression softened slightly. "I am Valyron, a sorcerer. I seek an ancient artifact hidden deep within this forest. But judging by your appearance, you're on a quest of your own. Perhaps we could help each other."

Leo's curiosity piqued. He had heard tales of sorcerers and their quests, but meeting one in the flesh was a different experience. "I'm Leo, a knight in search of my own destiny. And right now, that destiny seems to be leading me straight into trouble."

Valyron studied Leo for a moment, recognizing the determination in his eyes. "Trouble has a way of finding those who seek something greater. Perhaps our goals are not so different after all."

Before Leo could respond, a sudden, guttural roar erupted from the forest, sending a shiver down both their spines. The sound was followed by a tremor that shook the ground beneath their feet. Valyron and Leo exchanged a quick glance, realizing that whatever was causing this disturbance was close.

"Looks like we don't have much time," Valyron said, his voice firm. "Shall we face whatever this is together?"

Leo nodded, gripping his sword tightly. "Agreed. Let's see what this forest has in store for us."

As they ventured deeper into the forest, the once familiar surroundings grew increasingly alien. The trees seemed to close in around them, their branches twisting into grotesque shapes. Shadows danced across the forest floor, and the air grew thick with an oppressive, almost tangible, sense of dread.

The ground beneath them began to shift, revealing hidden traps and pitfalls. Valyron's staff glowed brighter as he murmured an incantation, revealing concealed hazards and illuminating their path. Leo's keen senses and swift reflexes proved invaluable as he deftly navigated the treacherous terrain, clearing a path for both of them.

A Clash in the Shadowed Grove

Finally, they reached a clearing where the source of the disturbance was revealed. A massive, twisted creature emerged from the shadows, its eyes burning with a malevolent fire. The beast, an amalgamation of various nightmarish features, was clearly not of this world.

Valyron stepped forward, his staff raised, and began to chant an incantation. The staff's crystal orb flared with intense light, casting a barrier around them. Leo, taking advantage of the distraction, charged at the creature, his sword cutting through the air with precision.

The battle that ensued was fierce and chaotic. The creature lunged at them with powerful swipes of its claws, its roar reverberating through the forest. Valyron's spells wove intricate patterns in the air, creating barriers and sending bolts of magical energy at their foe. Leo fought with a blend of grace and strength, his sword cleaving through the creature's defences.

Despite their combined efforts, the creature proved formidable. Valyron's spells seemed to weaken the beast, but it was Leo's unwavering resolve that tipped the scales. With a final, decisive strike, Leo plunged his sword into the creature's heart, ending the battle.

Breathing heavily, Leo and Valyron stood amidst the remnants of the beast, their eyes locked in mutual respect. The forest seemed to breathe a sigh of relief as the oppressive atmosphere lifted.

"Thank you for your help," Leo said, sheathing his sword. "I couldn't have done it without you."

Valyron nodded, his staff's glow dimming. "And I appreciate your assistance as well. It seems fate has brought us together for a reason."

As they prepared to continue their respective quests, the bond between them had solidified. They were no longer just two individuals lost in a forest; they were allies, bound by their shared experiences and the challenges that lay ahead.

With a newfound sense of purpose, Valyron and Leo set off once more, the forest behind them now a little less daunting. Their paths had converged, and together, they would face whatever challenges awaited them in the quest for their destinies.

5

ECHOES OF THE PAST

The hidden chamber beneath the pedestal was a vault of forgotten knowledge. Ancient scrolls lined the stone walls, their delicate paper yellowed with age, while enchanted artifacts lay scattered on shelves, glowing faintly with lingering magic. The air was heavy with the scent of old parchment, mingled with the subtle hum of mystical energy that seemed to pulse from every corner of the room.

The entrance to the chamber had been concealed for centuries, hidden beneath layers of earth and stone. Now, as Valyron and Leo descended the spiral staircase, they could feel the weight of history pressing down on them. The echoes of those who had once walked these halls seemed to whisper in the shadows, their presence a reminder of the ancient power that had been sealed away.

Valyron and Leo stepped cautiously into the chamber, their eyes wide with wonder at the treasures laid before them. The secrets of this place had been locked away for centuries, and now they were the first to set foot here in who knew how long.

The light from their torches flickered across the walls, casting long shadows that danced eerily in the corners of the room. Valyron's heart raced as he took in the sight of the ancient relics. This place held more than just forgotten knowledge—it was a repository of power, and they had only scratched the surface.

Valyron approached a table covered in scrolls, his fingers tracing the intricate designs etched into the wood. His eyes fell on a particular scroll, its edges worn but the writing still legible. Carefully, he unrolled it and began to read.

"The Prophecy of the Firebird," Valyron murmured, his voice echoing in the chamber. "It speaks of a great power hidden deep within this forest. A power that could either save the kingdom or bring about its destruction."

Leo, meanwhile, was drawn to a small, ornate box resting on a pedestal in the corner of the room. Inside, he found a compass—an intricately designed relic with a needle that spun erratically before settling in one direction. As he held it, he felt a strange connection to the object, as if it were calling to him.

"What is that?" Valyron asked, glancing over at Leo.

"I'm not sure," Leo replied, turning the compass over in his hands. "But I think it's trying to lead us somewhere. Maybe it's connected to the power you just read about."

Valyron's brow furrowed as he considered the possibility. "It could be. The scroll mentions that the power is guarded by ancient forces. This compass might be our key to finding it."

Before they could ponder further, the chamber trembled. The faint hum of magic grew louder, and the artifacts on the shelves began to vibrate. The ground beneath them shook as if the chamber itself was awakening from a long slumber. From the shadows, figures emerged—forest spirits, their translucent forms shimmering with ethereal light. Their eyes glowed with a cold, otherworldly intensity, and their presence filled the chamber with an aura of danger.

The spirits were unlike anything they had encountered before. Their bodies were made of the very essence of the forest, and their movements were fluid and unnatural, like wisps of smoke swirling in the wind. They floated silently toward Valyron and Leo, their eyes fixed on the intruders who had dared to disturb the sanctity of the chamber.

Without warning, the spirits attacked, their movements swift and fluid. One spirit lunged at Valyron, its hands crackling with energy. Valyron raised his staff, casting a protective barrier just in time to deflect the attack. The force of the impact sent him stumbling back, but he quickly regained his footing.

"Leo! These spirits—" Valyron began, but his words were cut short as another spirit dove toward him. He barely had time to react, summoning a gust of wind with his staff to blow the creature back.

Leo, sword in hand, engaged another spirit. His blade passed through its form, but the spirit only flickered before reforming and retaliating with a blast of energy that sent him reeling. "These things don't die easily!" he shouted, gritting his teeth as he prepared for another strike.

The chamber was alive with energy now, the air crackling with magic as the spirits circled them. Valyron's mind raced as he tried to come up with a plan. These spirits weren't like the usual enemies they faced—physical attacks seemed to have little effect, and their magic was unlike anything he had encountered before.

"They're bound to this chamber by ancient magic," Valyron realized aloud. "We need to disrupt their connection to the artifacts!"

With that, Valyron focused his energy on the shelves of glowing relics. He chanted an incantation, and the runes on his staff flared with light. A wave of magical force swept through the chamber, shattering the relics and sending shards of energy spiralling into the air. The spirits shrieked in agony as their forms began to flicker and fade, their connection to the chamber severed.

Leo took advantage of the chaos, delivering a final blow that dissipated the last of the spirits. Breathing heavily, he sheathed his sword and looked around the now-quiet chamber. "That was... intense."

Valyron nodded, lowering his staff. "These spirits were ancient guardians. They protected this place for centuries, and they won't be the last challenge we face."

As the dust settled, the silence that followed was deafening. The chamber, once alive with energy, now felt empty, as if the spirits had taken with them the very soul of the place. But the artifacts remained, glowing faintly in the dim light, a testament to the power that still lingered here.

Leo wiped the sweat from his brow and glanced down at the compass in his hand. The needle pointed unwaveringly toward a single direction. He could feel it pulling him, drawing him toward something deeper within the forest. Whatever lay ahead, it was calling to him with a force that was impossible to ignore.

"What now?" Leo asked, his voice low.

Valyron stared at the compass for a long moment before speaking. "We can leave now, with the knowledge we've gained. Or we can follow the compass and see where it leads. But if we do, there's no turning back."

Leo's grip on the compass tightened. "We've come this far. I'm not turning back now."

Valyron nodded, a glint of determination in his eyes. "Then we press on. Whatever awaits us, we'll face it together."

As they prepared to leave, Valyron paused for a moment, glancing back at the chamber. Something about this place felt unfinished, as if there were still secrets waiting to be uncovered. But there was no time to dwell on it now. They had made their choice, and there was no turning back.

With that, they left the chamber behind, the secrets of the forest beckoning them forward. The trees loomed overhead, their branches intertwining like skeletal fingers as the path ahead grew darker and more uncertain. Yet with every step, the compass led them closer to the heart of the forest's magic—and to the destiny that awaited them both.

But even as they walked, a sense of unease settled over Valyron. The spirits they had fought were not mere obstacles; they were warnings, remnants of an ancient power that had been sealed away for a reason. And whatever lay at the end of the compass's path was not something to be taken lightly.

Valyron could feel the weight of his staff in his hand, the familiar warmth of the magic coursing through it. It had been passed down to him by his parents when he was fifteen—a symbol of their legacy, and of the responsibility that now rested on his shoulders. He had carried it with him through countless battles, but this time felt different. This time, the stakes were higher, and the consequences of failure could be catastrophic.

As they ventured deeper into the forest, Valyron's thoughts drifted to his parents, now long gone. He had always hoped to make them proud, to honour their memory by using his magic for good. But now, with the weight of the prophecy hanging over him, he couldn't shake the feeling that he was on the brink of something far greater than himself. And for the first time in a long while, he felt a flicker of doubt.

But there was no turning back. The compass pointed forward, and so would they.

6

THE FALLEN KING

Lucifer had always been different. As a child, he had grown up under the oppressive rule of the dark lords, watching his family and people bow to their cruel demands. The dark lords, were a group of a council situated in a region called Nether. His lineage was rooted in servitude, yet from a young age, Lucifer harboured a deep, simmering hatred for the dark lords' tyranny. While others in his family complied, he began to dream of rebellion. His desire to break free was not a choice—it was a necessity for survival.

By the time he reached adulthood, Lucifer had transformed into a powerful sorcerer, driven by the fire of resistance. His hatred fuelled his training, and with time, he mastered the arcane arts. But rebellion came at a cost.

Lucifer's uprising against the dark lords was swift and fierce. He gathered those who shared his hatred, mounting a relentless assault on their stronghold. For a time, it seemed victory was within reach. Lucifer struck down several of their strongest generals, leading his people to freedom. He became a leader—a symbol of hope and resistance.

But the dark lords retaliated with a force Lucifer had underestimated. They destroyed his kingdom, and in a final, desperate battle, he was defeated. Left alive as a mockery of the leader he once was, Lucifer was forced into hiding, haunted by his failure.

Now, Lucifer wandered the land, seeking a way to reclaim his strength and exact revenge on the dark lords. His once-proud visage was marred by scars, both physical and emotional, and the weight of his past failures pressed heavily upon him. Yet, even in his weakened state, the fire of rebellion still burned within him.

But the wounds inflicted by the dark lords were deep. Each step through the dense forest sent jolts of pain through his body. His strength was waning, and the dizziness of blood loss clouded his vision. Lucifer knew he couldn't last much longer without aid.

He stumbled forward, clutching his side where a gash from the final battle had never fully healed. His cloak was tattered, drenched in sweat and blood. Every breath was a struggle, a fight against the pain that threatened to consume him. But he couldn't stop. Not now. Not when hope was so close.

When Lucifer finally reached the clearing where Valyron and Leo had made camp, he collapsed to his knees, the last of his energy spent. His vision blurred, and for a moment, everything went black.

Valyron and Leo jumped to their feet at the sound of the collapse, weapons at the ready. But as they approached the figure lying motionless on the ground, Valyron's sharp eyes recognized the faint traces of arcane power surrounding him. This was no ordinary man.

"Stay back, Leo," Valyron said cautiously, kneeling beside the fallen sorcerer. He gently turned Lucifer over, revealing a face marred by scars and exhaustion. "He's wounded. Badly."

Lucifer's eyes fluttered open, barely able to focus on Valyron. His voice was hoarse and weak. "I... need your help... please."

Valyron nodded, reaching into his satchel for a small vial of glowing liquid. "Drink this," he instructed, lifting Lucifer's head and pouring the potion between his cracked lips. The healing magic worked quickly, knitting together the worst of his wounds, though it couldn't fully restore his strength.

Lucifer coughed weakly as the potion took effect, his breathing becoming steadier, though he remained too weak to stand. "Thank... you..."

Leo stood watchfully nearby, his brow furrowed in concern. "Who is he? And why did he collapse here, of all places?"

Valyron's gaze softened as he sensed the depth of the man's despair. "I don't know yet... but he's no enemy. Let him rest. We'll get answers soon enough."

The Fallen King

For several hours, Lucifer lay in silence, recovering his strength. The potion had dulled the pain, but it couldn't erase the emotional scars that weighed heavily on his heart. When he finally spoke again, his voice was little more than a whisper.

"My name is Lucifer, I was a rebel at my place: The Nether. I opposed the tyranny of dark lords. Hence, I fought against them." he began, his eyes distant as he relived the memories. "But the dark lords… they took everything from me. My people, my kingdom… my pride." He swallowed hard, the taste of defeat bitter on his tongue. "Wait," said Leo. "You are the one who fought against the dark lords! I have heard stories of you. You were like a fairytale to me."

"I tried to fight them… but I wasn't strong enough."

Valyron listened intently, his expression compassionate. "You fought against the dark lords? Alone?"

Lucifer nodded weakly. "Yes, I thought I could stop them… but I was a fool. They crushed me. And now… I'm nothing more than a broken man, wandering the world… searching for a way to make things right."

Leo's doubt melted into empathy as he knelt beside the fallen king. "You've been through hell," he said softly. "But you're not alone anymore. We've fought our own battles, too. Maybe together… we can stand a chance."

Lucifer's eyes filled with tears, the weight of his failures pressing down on him. "I don't know if I'm strong enough anymore… I've lost so much."

Valyron placed a reassuring hand on his shoulder. "Strength isn't just about power. It's about endurance. The fact that you're still here, still fighting… that shows strength. And if you're willing to stand with us, we'll fight with you."

Lucifer looked between the two men, their words stirring something within him. For the first time in years, he felt a flicker of hope. "I'll fight," he whispered. "For justice… not for vengeance. I'll fight for something greater than myself."

With their alliance forged, Valyron helped Lucifer to his feet, though Lucifer still leaned heavily on him for support. "Rest for now," Valyron said. "You'll need your strength for what's to come."

And so, as the sun dipped below the horizon, the three of them—Lucifer, Valyron, and Leo—prepared for the battles that lay ahead. Though the scars of the past still lingered, they faced the future together, bound by their shared purpose.

But the dark lords would not rest. Even now, in the shadows, they plotted their next move. And this time, they would not be so easily defeated.

7

THE FORTRESS OF SHADOW AND LIGHT

*T*he wind whispered through the trees as the trio sat around a crackling fire in their camp. Leo and Valyron were discussing plans to fortify their position when Lucifer spoke up, his voice heavy with the weight of his thoughts.

"This camp... it won't protect us," Lucifer said, his gaze distant, as if he could see dangers lurking just beyond the forest. His hand subconsciously brushed over the scar that stretched across his chest, a painful reminder of his defeat. "We need more than a camp. We need something that can stand against the dark lords when they come for us."

Leo and Valyron exchanged glances. They knew Lucifer was right. Their makeshift camp might be sufficient for now, but it wouldn't hold against a determined assault from the dark lords' forces. Still, the idea of building a kingdom, something substantial, felt daunting.

"What do you suggest?" Valyron asked, his voice calm but laced with curiosity. He tapped the staff that had been passed down to him by his parents, feeling the familiar hum of magic coursing through it.

Lucifer looked up, a flicker of something—determination, or perhaps desperation—lighting his eyes. "I'll build us a fortress," he said, his voice firmer now. "A place that can withstand anything the dark lords throw at us."

Valyron raised an eyebrow. "With what resources? We've been scouring the area for days, and nothing here can sustain a fortress, let alone one strong enough to defend against them."

Lucifer stood, his tall frame casting a long shadow over the fire. "Not with resources," he said quietly, "with power."

Before either of them could protest, Lucifer stepped away from the campfire. He closed his eyes, and the air around him began to shimmer with energy. The ground trembled beneath their feet as Lucifer's magic surged through the earth, drawing on ancient forces that lay dormant beneath the forest floor.

Leo and Valyron watched in awe as stone walls began to rise from the ground, twisting and forming into towers and battlements. The castle was unlike anything they had ever seen—dark and imposing yet somehow elegant. It was not a fortress of despair but one of resilience. The walls glistened as if imbued with a protective enchantment, and as the final stones locked into place, a magical barrier shimmered around it, almost invisible to the naked eye.

When it was done, Lucifer staggered, his breath ragged. His usually confident stance wavered as he struggled to keep himself upright. Valyron quickly approached, offering him support.

"Lucifer," Valyron said, concern etched in his voice. "You used dark magic, didn't you? After everything you've been through... are you still tied to the dark lords?"

Lucifer shook his head, though his gaze remained fixed on the fortress. "No, Valyron. This is not their magic." He paused, drawing in a deep breath. "It's my power. The remnants of what I once was—a leader. I didn't need their darkness to build this. I needed to remember who I am."

He looked at Valyron, his eyes filled with a mix of pain and defiance. "But I can't lie to myself. Using magic like this... it brings me closer to them. Closer to what I could have been if I had stayed with them."

Leo, who had been silent until now, stepped forward. "So, you're saying this fortress... it's a reminder of your past? A past you rejected?" His voice was softer than usual, and for a moment, the tension in the air seemed to ease.

Lucifer nodded. "I was born into a family that served the dark lords. For years, I was blind to the cruelty around me, raised to believe their lies. But as I grew older, I saw the truth. I saw the suffering they caused, the despair they revelled in. I couldn't stand by and let it continue."

His voice trembled as he continued, the words heavy with emotion. "I turned against them. Betrayed everything I knew, everything I had been taught. I fought for justice. For freedom. I became a leader—a powerful one. But it wasn't enough. They defeated me, humiliated me. I failed."

Lucifer's hands clenched into fists, his knuckles white against his skin. "And now... I'm here. Wounded, weakened, but still fighting. Because if I don't, then everything I've done will have been for nothing."

Valyron placed a hand on Lucifer's shoulder. "You're not alone in this. You made this fortress with your power, not theirs. That means something. And we're here to help you. We trust you."

Lucifer looked at Valyron, and for the first time in a long while, a flicker of hope crossed his face. "Thank you," he said quietly. "But I can't shake the fear that one day, I might lose control. That the darkness might creep back in."

Leo smirked, trying to lighten the mood. "Then we'll just have to keep an eye on you, won't we? Besides, if you go all dark lord on us, Valyron here will just blast you with one of his spells."

Lucifer let out a small, almost reluctant laugh. "I'd like to see him try."

They shared a brief moment of camaraderie before the seriousness of their situation returned. The fortress was built, but their journey was far from over. The dark lords were still out there, and they would come for them eventually. But now, they had a place to make their stand—a fortress of shadows and light.

As they prepared to rest for the night, Lucifer couldn't help but gaze at the castle he had created. It was a symbol of his past, but also of his future. A future where he would fight, not just for himself, but for those who stood by his side.

For now, they were safe. But in the distance, the shadows stirred, and the dark lords were watching.

8

SHADOW AND FIRE

The morning sun filtered through the dense canopy of the enchanted forest, casting intricate patterns of light and shadow on the forest floor. Valyron and Leo, having just finished discussing their plans for the defence of the newly built castle, were preparing for the arrival of Lucifer's pet dragon, Draco. The anticipation was palpable, as the creature's reputation preceded it.

Lucifer, though visibly weary and battered from his recent battles, maintained an air of regal authority as he directed the final touches on the castle. His face, marked by scars and the weight of past defeats, held a mixture of determination and sorrow. He was resolute in his mission to aid Valyron and Leo, yet the burden of his past victories and losses seemed to press heavily upon him.

The silence was broken by the distant rumble of wings. Draco, the hybrid dragon, emerged from the shadows, its imposing figure a blend of various dragon types. Its body, dark and shadowy like a shadow dragon, was interspersed with elements of fire, ice, and storm. The dragon's appearance was both awe-inspiring and unnerving, its scales shifting colours in the play of light and shadow.

Valyron and Leo watched in amazement as Draco landed gracefully, despite its formidable size. The ground trembled slightly beneath the dragon's massive claws, and the air crackled with residual energy from its flight. The contrast between Draco's shadowy form and the shimmering light of the morning sun created a striking, almost surreal image.

Lucifer approached Draco with a mixture of pride and weariness. "Draco," he said, his voice carrying both authority and affection, "meet Valyron and Leo. They have been instrumental in our efforts to secure a safe haven for the forces we've gathered."

Shadow and Fire

Draco's eyes, glowing with an otherworldly light, scanned Valyron and Leo with an intelligent curiosity. The dragon's scales shimmered with hues of black, red, blue, and silver, reflecting its unique blend of dragon types. It was a magnificent, if somewhat intimidating, sight.

Valyron stepped forward, his eyes reflecting both respect and intrigue. "I've heard tales of such a creature, but seeing Draco in person is a different experience entirely. His presence alone seems to shift the very air around us."

Leo nodded in agreement, his gaze fixed on Draco with a mix of admiration and wariness. "What kind of dragon is he? I've heard legends, but this... this is beyond anything I've imagined."

Lucifer, with a pained smile, began to explain. "Draco is a unique amalgamation of various dragon types, each contributing to his extraordinary abilities. His body, however, is that of a shadow dragon, which allows him to blend into darkness and manipulate shadows. The fire, ice, and storm elements you see are the result of ancient rituals and the merging of different dragon essences."

As Lucifer spoke, Draco moved with a fluid grace, its shadowy form gliding effortlessly across the landscape. The dragon's presence was a stark reminder of Lucifer's past and the sacrifices he had made. His loyalty to Draco was evident, a bond forged through years of shared battles and struggles.

Leo, sensing the weight of Lucifer's words, spoke with compassion. "You've gone through so much, Lucifer. The loss of your kingdom, the battles you fought... it must have been incredibly difficult."

Lucifer's gaze grew distant, his eyes reflecting a deep sadness. "It was a time of great pain and loss. My kingdom was once a beacon of hope, but the dark lords' betrayal left it in ruins. I fought to protect it, but in the end, I was left defeated and wounded. Draco and I have been on the run, seeking allies and ways to reclaim what was lost."

Valyron, moved by Lucifer's words, stepped closer. "You don't have to carry this burden alone. We understand the weight of loss and the struggle for redemption. We're here to help you, and Draco will be a valuable ally in our fight."

Lucifer's eyes softened, a glimmer of hope breaking through his weariness. "Thank you, Valyron. Your support means more than you know. Draco and I have been through many trials, and knowing that we are not alone in this fight brings some solace."

Draco approached, lowering its massive head as if acknowledging the shared sentiment. The dragon's eyes, though fierce, held a flicker of gentleness as it regarded Valyron and Leo. The connection between the dragon and its master was evident in the mutual trust and understanding they shared.

As the day progressed, Lucifer and his companions prepared the castle for the arrival of the forces that would soon join their cause. Draco's presence brought a sense of security and power, and the castle, though not a dark fortress, was fortified with numerous traps and defences. The blend of shadow and light in its design reflected the balance between hope and vigilance.

Valyron, Leo, and Lucifer worked together, their efforts complemented by Draco's keen instincts and abilities. The castle took shape, its walls imbued with a sense of resilience and strength. The landscape, once marked by struggle and conflict, began to transform into a bastion of hope and determination.

As the sun dipped below the horizon, casting a golden glow over the castle, the group gathered to reflect on their progress. The castle, now a symbol of their combined efforts, stood as a testament to their resolve and unity.

Lucifer, though still bearing the marks of his past battles, appeared more at ease. The support of Valyron and Leo, along with the presence of Draco, had rekindled a glimmer of hope within him. He knew that the road ahead would be fraught with challenges, but the bonds forged in the face of adversity had given him renewed strength.

As the evening settled in, the group gathered around a fire, sharing stories and plans for the future. The warmth of the fire and the camaraderie of the moment provided a brief respite from the struggles they had endured. It was a moment of reflection and anticipation, a chance to regroup and prepare for the challenges yet to come.

The chapter concluded with a sense of cautious optimism. The castle, though still in the early stages of its transformation, stood as a beacon of hope and resilience. The presence of Draco and the unwavering support of Valyron and Leo gave Lucifer a renewed sense of purpose. The journey ahead was uncertain, but the strength of their unity and the echoes of the past guided their path forward.

9

THE GATHERING STORM

The dawn broke over the horizon, casting its first golden rays on the newly established castle, now a formidable bastion of hope and strength. Within its fortified walls, preparations for the impending battle were in full swing. The castle, now a symbol of resilience, was abuzz with activity as the forces gathered to face the looming threat.

Valyron, Leo, and Lucifer stood atop a rise overlooking the bustling camp below. The scene was one of organized chaos, with soldiers, craftsmen, and mages working tirelessly. The castle grounds were transformed into a hive of activity, as every corner of the fortress was dedicated to the preparation for war.

"We have to ensure that everything is in place before the enemy arrives," Valyron said, his voice carrying a note of urgency as he surveyed the scene. His staff, a symbol of his magical prowess, was ever at his side, glowing with a faint, reassuring light.

Leo, his gaze fixed on the training grounds where soldiers practiced their skills, nodded in agreement. "We need to make sure our troops are not only well-equipped but also well-trained. This is a battle that will test every ounce of their resolve."

Lucifer, though still bearing the marks of his past battles, was deeply involved in the planning and coordination of the forces. His authority and experience brought a level of organization to the preparations. "We must forge alliances and strengthen our defence. The dark lords will not be easily defeated. Our army must be ready for any challenge."

The Gathering Storm

As the sun climbed higher in the sky, the camp below continued to grow. Soldiers from various regions and backgrounds had answered the call to arms, each bringing their own skills and expertise. The army's formation was a testament to the unity and strength of the diverse forces now gathered.

The camp was divided into several sections: the barracks for rest and strategy discussions, the forges where weapons were crafted, the apothecary where potions and magical brews were prepared, and the training grounds where soldiers honed their skills.

The barracks were filled with soldiers discussing tactics and sharing stories of past battles. From seasoned warriors to young recruits, the atmosphere was one of camaraderie and determination. They were united by a common goal and a shared commitment to the cause.

In the forges, the air was thick with the smell of burning coal and the clanging of metal. Blacksmiths worked tirelessly, shaping swords, spears, and shields. The weapons were crafted with precision and care, each one imbued with protective enchantments and forged to withstand the dark lords' formidable forces.

"The quality of these weapons is crucial," said one of the lead blacksmiths, as he examined a newly forged sword. "We need to ensure that they are not only sharp but also resilient. The dark lords' minions are known for their strength and cunning."

The blacksmiths worked alongside mages who enhanced the weapons with magical runes. Each rune was carefully inscribed to grant the weapons additional power and durability. The synergy between the blacksmiths and mages was a vital aspect of the preparations, ensuring that the army would be well-equipped for the upcoming battle.

In the apothecary, the scent of various herbs and concoctions filled the air. Alchemists and mages worked together to brew potions and prepare spells. Healing potions, strength elixirs, and enchantments were created with meticulous attention to detail.

"We need to ensure that we have enough potions to last through the battle and beyond," said an alchemist, carefully measuring ingredients for a healing brew. "The soldiers will need to be in peak condition, and these potions will be essential for their recovery."

Spells were also prepared, each one designed to offer protection, enhance abilities, or provide strategic advantages. The mages worked diligently, channelling their energy into creating powerful enchantments that would bolster the army's effectiveness.

The training grounds were a hive of activity, with soldiers engaging in combat drills and strategic exercises. The sound of clashing swords, the rhythm of archery practice, and the coordination of formations filled the air. Experienced trainers led the sessions, imparting their knowledge and skills to the recruits.

Leo observed the training with a critical eye. "We need to make sure our soldiers are not only skilled in combat but also able to work together as a cohesive unit. This battle will require precise coordination and strategy."

Valyron, using his magical abilities, provided support and guidance. He enhanced the training exercises with illusions and magical obstacles, creating scenarios that tested the soldiers' adaptability and problem-solving skills. "It's essential that they can think on their feet and react to unexpected challenges," he explained.

The army was composed of a diverse range of individuals, each contributing their unique skills. There were infantry soldiers, archers, cavalry units, dragon warriors, healers, mages, illusionists and so many more, each playing a critical role in the overall strategy. The diversity of the forces was both a strength and a challenge, requiring careful coordination and communication.

Lucifer, with his strategic mind, worked on integrating the various units into a cohesive force. "We need to use our strengths to our advantage. The dark lords are formidable opponents, but our combined forces give us a unique edge. We must leverage our diversity to outmanoeuvre and overpower them."

As the preparations neared completion, the focus shifted to the strategic deployment of the army. Maps and charts were spread across tables as Valyron, Leo, and Lucifer discussed their approach.

"We need to be ready for a multi-front assault," Valyron said, pointing to different locations on the map. "We'll position our forces to cover key strategic points and anticipate possible routes of attack."

Leo added, "We should use the terrain to our advantage. The forest can be both a barrier and an asset. We can set up ambushes and use the natural cover to surprise the enemy."

Lucifer nodded in agreement. "We also need to be prepared for deception. The dark lords are known for their cunning tactics. We must anticipate their moves and counter them effectively."

As night fell, the camp was illuminated by the glow of lanterns and the flickering of torches. The soldiers gathered for a final briefing before the battle, their faces reflecting a mix of determination and apprehension.

Valyron, Leo, and Lucifer addressed the troops, their words inspiring and motivating. "We stand on the brink of a pivotal moment," Valyron began. "Our unity and strength will be tested, but together, we can overcome any challenge."

Leo continued, "Remember why we fight. Each of you plays a crucial role in this battle. Your courage and skill will make the difference."

Lucifer concluded, "We have come a long way, and we have prepared as thoroughly as possible. Trust in each other, trust in our strategy, and let's face the darkness with unwavering resolve."

As the troops prepared for the battle ahead, a sense of purpose and unity enveloped the camp. The next day would bring the clash of armies, but for now, the focus was on readiness and resolve. The gathering storm was about to break, and the forces within the castle were prepared to face it with strength and determination.

The Fate of the Fallen

The army readied itself for the battle that lay ahead, the castle standing as a symbol of their collective strength and resolve. The preparations had been thorough, and the strategy was set. All that remained was to face the darkness and fight for their future.

10

THE DAWN OF RECKONING

The horizon blazed with hues of red and orange as dawn's first light touched the fortified castle of Valyron, Leo, and Lucifer. The night had been restless for the army; the upcoming confrontation with the dark lords loomed heavily over them. The preparations were complete, and now the time had come to execute the meticulously crafted strategy.

Valyron and Leo stood on a raised platform overlooking the sprawling battlefield that lay before them. The castle, a testament to Lucifer's formidable magic, had been fortified with traps and enchantments. It was a stronghold designed not just for defence but for offensive manoeuvres as well.

"We've been through hell to get here," Leo said, his voice steady but carrying an undertone of tension. "Now it's time to make it all worth it."

Valyron, his staff glowing with latent power, nodded in agreement. "The dark lords will underestimate us if we show weakness. Every detail must be executed flawlessly."

The army had been divided into several units, each with specific roles and positions. On the left flank, archers and mages were stationed behind a series of magical barriers designed to absorb and deflect enemy projectiles. They were positioned to launch a barrage of arrows and spells as soon as the dark lords' forces advanced.

To the right, heavily armoured infantry units, equipped with reinforced shields and swords, formed a solid line. Behind them were siege engines, ready to unleash destruction upon the enemy. These soldiers had trained rigorously, their movements synchronized to perfection.

In the centre of the formation, a battalion of elite warriors, each skilled in both combat and magic, prepared to engage the dark lords directly. Their leader, a fierce warrior named Kael, adjusted his armour and glanced at Valyron for confirmation.

"Everything's set, Valyron," Kael called out, his voice carrying over the noise of the bustling army.

"Good," Valyron replied. "Hold the line and stay vigilant. We need to hold our ground until Leo and I can press the advantage."

As the sun climbed higher, the distant rumble of the dark lords' army became audible. A dark cloud of smoke and dust marked their approach, a foreboding sign of the coming onslaught. The ground shook under the weight of their approach, and the sky was darkened by the silhouette of the dark lords' monstrous war machines.

"Prepare for battle!" Lucifer's voice boomed, echoing through the castle. "Our time has come. For those who fight bravely, glory and freedom await. For those who falter, the darkness will consume you!"

The army's anticipation reached a fever pitch as the dark lords' forces appeared in full view. The dark lords' standard-bearers marched at the head of their legions, their banners snapping ominously in the wind. War cries and the clash of metal filled the air as they prepared to engage.

"Forward, my minions!" roared the lead dark lord, a figure cloaked in black armour. "Let the world tremble at our might. Crush these rebels and let no mercy be shown!"

The ground shook as the dark lords' forces surged forward. The dark lords themselves, figures of menacing power, led their troops with unwavering authority. The clash of steel and the shouts of warriors filled the battlefield as the two armies collided. Valyron's elite warriors fought with precision and power, their magical abilities enhancing their physical attacks. The ground was littered with the fallen as both sides fought tooth and nail for every inch of territory.

"Hold steady!" Valyron shouted to the archers. "Aim for their siege engines! We need to neutralize their long-range capabilities!"

Leo, on the right flank, directed the infantry and siege engines. The heavy units braced themselves as the dark lords' forces charged. The siege engines roared to life, launching boulders and fireballs into the enemy ranks, creating chaos and disruption.

"Advance, but stay close!" Leo commanded his troops. "We can't afford to be overwhelmed. Focus on breaking their lines and pushing them back!"

The siege engines fired again and again, hurling massive projectiles into the dark lords' ranks. Explosions of light and bursts of energy lit up the battlefield as spells collided with enemy formations. The archers and mages on the left flank fired a relentless volley of arrows and spells, creating a barrier of magical and physical projectiles that forced the advancing dark lords to slow their advance.

"Fire, now!" the dark lord general barked, raising his sword high. "Destroy their defence and break their spirit!"

Meanwhile, Lucifer and Draco soared above the battlefield. The dragon's breath of dark flames seared through the enemy ranks, creating a path of destruction. Draco's ability to shift between various dragon forms allowed him to adapt to different combat scenarios, whether unleashing torrents of fire or summoning dark storms.

"Prepare to unleash hell!" Lucifer roared, rallying the troops. "For every soul lost, for every tear shed, we will make them pay!"

Draco's fiery breath incinerated enemy war machines and troops alike, while Lucifer's dark magic created storms and lightning that struck fear into the enemy forces. The sky itself seemed to writhe with the intensity of the battle, adding to the chaos below.

Lucifer's eyes blazed with determination as he guided Draco's assault. "Burn their siege towers! Break their will to fight!" He directed Draco to unleash a torrent of flames upon the enemy's siege engines, melting the metal and sending shockwaves through their ranks.

Draco's dark wings flapped with immense power, sending gusts of wind and debris swirling across the battlefield. The combination of Draco's fiery attacks and Lucifer's dark magic created a scene of apocalyptic destruction.

As the dark lords' forces began to retreat, Valyron and Leo saw an opportunity to push forward. The ground commanders, their faces grim with the weight of battle, led their troops in a concerted push against the retreating enemy.

Valyron's staff crackled with energy as he unleashed a series of powerful spells, creating barriers of light that protected his soldiers while simultaneously launching devastating attacks at the dark lords' rear guard.

"Advance, now!" Valyron shouted, his voice barely audible over the roar of combat. "They're breaking! Press the advantage!"

Leo, leading the charge, fought with a fierce intensity. His blade, glowing with magical energy, cut through the dark lords' defence. He moved with precision and skill, rallying his troops with each swing of his sword.

"Keep pushing!" Leo yelled, sweat and blood mingling on his face. "We've got them on the run! Finish this!"

As the sun began to set, casting a warm glow over the battlefield, the dark lords' forces were driven back. The ground was strewn with the remnants of the battle, but the castle stood resilient, a symbol of their hard-won victory.

Lucifer descended from the sky, Draco landing gracefully beside him. The wounded leader looked out over the battlefield with a mix of relief and exhaustion. His once pristine armour was now battered and scorched, and his expression was one of solemn victory.

"We've done it," Lucifer said, his voice weary but filled with pride. "The dark lords have been pushed back. We may have won this battle but the fight is far from over."

The Dawn of Reckoning

Valyron and Leo joined Lucifer, their expressions reflecting the weight of their victory and the cost it had come with. They took in the devastation, their hearts heavy with the knowledge of the lives lost.

"The battle is won, but we must remain vigilant. The war is over for now," Valyron said, his gaze steady. "This is only the beginning of our fight."

Leo nodded in agreement. "We've proven our strength today. Let's use this victory to forge a future where we're no longer under threat."

As the soldiers began to regroup and tend to the wounded, the atmosphere was filled with a sense of accomplishment and the knowledge that their journey was far from over. The preparations had led to this pivotal moment, and the alliances forged in battle would shape the future of their land.

The victors of the day looked toward the horizon, ready to face whatever challenges lay ahead. Their unity and determination had carried them through the trials of the day, and they stood poised to confront whatever lay in their path.

As the night fell and the stars began to appear, the flickering torches cast long shadows over the battlefield, highlighting the cost of their hard-won victory. The air was thick with the smoke of battle and the scent of burning debris. The soldiers, though weary and battered, felt a renewed sense of purpose.

And so, with the echoes of the battle still ringing in their ears, the heroes prepared for the trials yet to come, knowing that their fight was far from over. Their resolve was unshakable, and their hearts were set on ensuring that the darkness that had once threatened their world would never return...

11

THE DARK KNIGHT RISES

The aftermath of the battle left a sense of uneasy calm over the land. The dark lords had been repelled, their forces scattered, but the scars of conflict were still fresh. Lucifer, despite his wounds, stood at the forefront of the victory celebrations, his resolve unwavering. The once-turbulent skies were now a canvas of hope, and Lucifer's gaze swept over the gathered heroes and soldiers.

Valyron, Leo, and Kael were at the centre of the assembly, their faces a mixture of exhaustion and relief. The battle had tested their limits, but they had emerged victorious. The air was filled with the sounds of celebration, but Lucifer's attention was drawn to the trio.

"Valyron," Lucifer began, his voice carrying the weight of gratitude and respect. "Your bravery and intellect have proven invaluable. Leo, your strength and leadership on the battlefield have been nothing short of extraordinary. And Kael," he paused, looking at the veteran warrior, "your unwavering commitment to our cause has been a beacon of hope."

The trio stood in respectful silence as Lucifer continued. "As a token of my gratitude, I wish to offer each of you a place in my court. Valyron, your unique intellect and elegance will be a great asset as my Minister. Leo, with your prowess and reliability, I would be honoured to have you as the Chief of Army. And Kael," Lucifer's gaze softened, "your role in this victory deserves recognition, I would like to have you as the Military General of my Army."

Kael's expression remained stoic, though a hint of reluctance lingered in his eyes. "My place is not here, Lucifer," Kael replied firmly. "There is someone else who would be a worthy addition to your ranks."

Lucifer's curiosity was piqued. "Who might that be?"

Kael's gaze shifted towards Leo and Valyron. "Apex," he said. "He has proven himself time and again, and I believe he would fit well within your ranks."

The suggestion was met with nods of approval from Leo and Valyron. "Truly, Apex deserves this opportunity," Leo agreed. "He has shown remarkable skill and courage."

Lucifer nodded, his expression thoughtful. "Very well. I will extend my offer to Apex then."

Apex, who had been standing at the edge of the assembly, approached with a mixture of anticipation and trepidation. Lucifer's eyes assessed him with a mix of curiosity and respect.

"Apex," Lucifer addressed him, "your skills and bravery have not gone unnoticed. I would like to offer you a position in my army. Your valour on the battlefield speaks volumes."

Apex's eyes widened, and he bowed respectfully. "I accept your offer, my lord."

As the new roles were assigned, Lucifer began to share more about his vision for the future. "With this new dawn, we shall build a kingdom that stands as a testament to our strength and unity. Valyron, as Minister, your counsel will guide us through the trials ahead. Leo, as Chief of Army, you will lead our forces with honour and strategy. And Apex, your dedication will fortify our ranks."

The trio accepted their roles with a mixture of pride and responsibility. The road ahead was uncertain, but their purpose was clear.

Lucifer then turned to Valyron, his gaze earnest. "Your staff, Valyron. I have heard its significance. It represents more than just power; it symbolizes your journey and the sacrifices you have made."

Valyron nodded, his grip tightening around the staff. "It is a reminder of my past and my promise to honour it."

Lucifer's expression softened. "We all have our pasts, and it is through our struggles that we find our true strength. We will forge a new future together, one that acknowledges our sacrifices and celebrates our victories." He later adds," My dear Noblemen, please do meet me tomorrow. I have some surprises for the three of you."

The celebration continued, and the kingdom began to take shape. The castle, built by Lucifer's dark powers but designed to be a bastion of hope rather than fear, stood as a symbol of the new era. It was not a place of darkness but a stronghold of safety and security.

As the sun set on the horizon, casting a golden glow over the land, the heroes looked towards the future with a sense of renewed purpose. The battle had been won, but the journey was far from over. Together, they would face the challenges ahead, their unity a testament to their shared resolve.

And so, amidst the echoes of victory and the promise of a new beginning, Lucifer now became a king. Valyron, Leo, and Apex prepared to embrace their new roles, knowing that their combined strength would shape the destiny of their world.

12

THE GIFT OF GRATITUDE

The kingdom was healing, slowly regaining its strength after the devastation of war. The new castle stood as a testament to their resilience, but the battle scars ran deep within the hearts of its defenders. Leo, Valyron, and Apex were adjusting to their new roles within Lucifer's court, but the weight of responsibility hung heavily on their shoulders. Each day brought new challenges, and every victory felt bittersweet.

But amidst the turmoil, Lucifer knew his companions deserved more than just titles. He gathered them in the grand hall, where the flickering torches cast long shadows against the stone walls. The air was thick with anticipation as they stood before him.

"I wanted to thank you all properly for your loyalty, your bravery," Lucifer began, his voice reverberating through the chamber. "What you have done for this kingdom cannot be repaid with words alone."

A faint smile crossed Leo's lips. "You've already given us more than we could ask for, Lucifer."

Lucifer shook his head. "No, my friend. I have one more gift for each of you—something that will strengthen our bond and give you the power to protect this kingdom even further."

With a wave of his hand, the massive doors behind them creaked open. A gust of wind swept into the hall, carrying with it the sound of beating wings. The room darkened momentarily as three large, majestic dragons entered, each one embodying a different element and personality.

Leo's eyes widened as he gazed upon the magnificent creatures. "Dragons…"

"Yes," Lucifer said with a grin. "These are not just any dragons. They have been bonded to you, chosen based on your strengths, your essence."

The first dragon stepped forward toward Leo. Its scales shimmered in hues of silver and blue, and lightning sparked from its wings as it moved. This was an elemental dragon, fierce and unpredictable, much like Leo himself. The dragon lowered its head to Leo, who extended his hand cautiously. When his hand touched the dragon's snout, a surge of energy passed between them, a connection that went beyond words.

"For you, Leo," Lucifer said. "An elemental dragon, powerful and adaptable, just like you."

Leo felt the weight of responsibility lift slightly as he gazed into the dragon's eyes. He had been given a new companion, one that would fight alongside him, not just with strength, but with the force of nature itself.

Next, Valyron's dragon approached. Its body was a deep shade of black, with hints of violet running along its scales. It was a shadow dragon, mysterious and elusive, much like Valyron. The dragon's eyes gleamed with ancient knowledge, and when it stood before Valyron, it seemed to blend into the darkness itself.

"For you, Valyron," Lucifer said softly. "A shadow dragon, one that mirrors your intellect and mastery of the unknown."

Valyron bowed slightly to the creature before extending his hand, feeling the cold, calming energy that the dragon radiated. It wasn't just a beast—it was a guardian of secrets, one that would protect him in ways no one else could.

Finally, Apex's dragon came forward. It was a massive, fire-breathing creature with scales that glowed like molten lava. This dragon embodied raw strength and fury, a perfect reflection of Apex's warrior spirit. Apex didn't hesitate as he approached the dragon, meeting its fiery gaze with his own.

"For you, Apex," Lucifer said, his voice filled with pride. "A fire dragon, fierce and unyielding, just like you."

The Gift of Gratitude

Apex smiled, feeling a deep connection with the creature. This dragon wasn't just a weapon; it was a symbol of his own journey—a journey that had been filled with hardship and battles. Apex had come from nothing, a nameless soldier who had clawed his way up through the ranks with sheer determination and strength. He had been a loner, always fighting for survival in a world that showed him no mercy. But now, he had found a place where he belonged, and this dragon was the final piece that completed him.

As the three men bonded with their dragons, they felt a new sense of purpose—a renewed determination to protect the kingdom from whatever threats lay ahead. They were no longer just soldiers; they were dragon riders, the defenders of the realm.

Lucifer watched them with a sense of satisfaction. These were no ordinary warriors—they were legends in the making.

But before they could settle into their new roles, an urgent message arrived. Scouts had spotted a nearby village being plundered by looters. The peace they had fought so hard to secure was already being threatened.

Without hesitation, Leo, Valyron, and Apex mounted their dragons. The bond between rider and dragon was instantaneous, and as they took to the skies, they felt the power of their new companions surging through them. The wind whipped past them as they soared over the kingdom, their eyes scanning the landscape below.

The village came into view, and the scene was one of chaos. Buildings were burning, and villagers were fleeing in all directions as the looters tore through the town, taking everything they could get their hands on.

"We need to stop them before they destroy everything," Leo shouted over the roar of the wind.

Valyron nodded, his eyes narrowing as he surveyed the situation. "We'll take them by surprise. Apex, you and your dragon can drive them out with fire. Leo, you and I will handle the rest."

Apex grinned, eager to put his dragon's power to the test. With a command, his fire dragon swooped down toward the village, unleashing a torrent of flames that sent the looters scattering. The sheer force of the attack was enough to break their formation, and the looters began to flee in panic.

Leo and Valyron followed close behind, their dragons descending with precision and grace. Leo's elemental dragon summoned a storm, rain and lightning striking down the fleeing looters, while Valyron's shadow dragon enveloped the remaining enemies in darkness, disorienting them and making them easy targets.

Within moments, the looters were defeated, and the village was saved. The villagers looked up in awe as the three dragon riders landed in the centre of the town, their dragons standing tall and proud beside them.

The village elder approached, his hands trembling as he bowed before them. "Thank you, brave warriors. You have saved us from certain doom."

Leo dismounted his dragon, offering the elder a reassuring smile. "We are here to protect the kingdom and its people. You are safe now."

Valyron and Apex joined him, their dragons standing watchful behind them. The bond between the three men had grown even stronger through this battle, and as they looked at the grateful faces of the villagers, they knew that their journey was far from over. There would be more battles to fight, more challenges to face, but with their dragons by their side, they felt unstoppable.

Lucifer had given them more than just a gift—he had given them the power to change the fate of the kingdom. And they intended to use that power to its fullest.

13

THE DARK COUNCIL

*T*he sun dipped below the horizon, casting long shadows across the fields where the armies had clashed. In the aftermath of battle, the campfires of Lucifer's forces flickered in the dark, their light struggling to dispel the lingering tension. Among the survivors, a palpable unease lingered—an anticipation of something darker yet to come.

Valyron and Leo stood side by side, surveying the camp. The men were weary, and though the battle had been won, there was a sense that this victory was only the beginning of something far more dangerous. Leo rested a hand on the hilt of his sword, eyes scanning the forest beyond the clearing.

"Do you feel it?" Leo asked quietly, his voice barely above a whisper.

Valyron nodded, clutching his staff tighter. "A storm is coming, and not the kind that brings rain."

Just then, a chill wind swept through the camp, extinguishing several fires. The warriors around them glanced up nervously, their hands instinctively moving toward their weapons. A strange mist began to roll in from the forest, creeping along the ground and swallowing the camp in an eerie silence.

From the depths of the mist, a figure emerged—a tall, imposing figure draped in dark robes. His eyes glowed with an unnatural light, and the ground beneath his feet seemed to wither with each step. This was not a mere soldier of the Dark Lords; this was a higher power, a member of the Dark Council itself, sent to exact vengeance for their fallen brethren.

"Who goes there?" Leo called out, drawing his sword, the blade shimmering in the dim light. Valyron stepped forward, his staff pulsing with arcane energy, ready to strike.

The figure halted at the edge of the camp, and a deep, resonant voice echoed through the mist. "I am Revenor, Herald of the Dark Council. You may have defeated our forces today, but you have yet to face true darkness."

Lucifer appeared beside Valyron and Leo, his dark cloak billowing in the wind. His eyes, though weary from battle, burned with a fierce determination. "Revenor," he spat, recognizing the name. "So, the Council sends their lapdog. Are they too afraid to face me themselves?"

Revenor's eyes narrowed, and a cruel smile twisted his lips. "You misunderstand, Lucifer. The Dark Council is not afraid of you—they simply see you as a nuisance, one that will soon be eradicated. I am here to deliver that judgment."

With a wave of Revenor's hand, the mist around them thickened, and from its depths, shadowy figures began to emerge—twisted, grotesque creatures forged from the darkest magic. They snarled and hissed, their glowing eyes fixed on the camp, eager for bloodshed.

Lucifer turned to Valyron and Leo, his expression grim. "Prepare yourselves. This will not be like the last battle. These creatures are born of pure darkness—they cannot be defeated by strength alone."

Leo gripped his sword tighter, his mind racing. "What are they?"

Valyron glanced at the creatures, his mind calculating. "They are beings of shadow and despair. Physical attacks won't be enough. We'll need to outsmart them."

The first wave of shadow creatures lunged toward them, and the camp exploded into chaos. Warriors rushed to defend themselves, but their weapons passed through the creatures as if they were striking air. Panic set in as men fell to the ground, their faces twisted in terror as the creatures drained the life from them.

"Fall back!" Leo shouted, trying to organize the scattered soldiers. "Form a defensive line!"

Valyron raised his staff, channelling his magic into a barrier of light that pushed back the encroaching shadows. "Light is their weakness! We need to hold them off until we can find a way to banish them!"

The Dark Council

Lucifer, meanwhile, summoned Draco. The massive dragon swooped down from the sky, its dark wings cutting through the mist. With a roar, Draco unleashed a torrent of flames, burning away several of the shadow creatures, but more quickly filled their place.

Revenor watched from the sidelines, his expression unreadable. "Do you see now, Lucifer? You cannot defeat what you do not understand. The darkness is eternal, and it will consume everything you hold dear."

Lucifer glared at Revenor, his anger barely contained. "You underestimate the power of light and hope."

Revenor sneered. "Hope is nothing more than a fleeting illusion. But if you're so confident, then let's see how long that hope lasts."

With that, Revenor raised his hands, and the ground beneath the camp began to tremble. From the earth, massive tendrils of dark energy erupted, wrapping themselves around the soldiers and dragging them into the ground. The cries of the men filled the air as they were consumed by the darkness.

Leo fought desperately, his sword glowing with elemental power as he struck at the tendrils, severing them and freeing the soldiers. But for every tendril he cut down, two more took its place. The battle was quickly becoming overwhelming.

Valyron, realizing that they were losing ground, turned to Lucifer. "We need to focus our efforts on Revenor! If we can break his connection to the darkness, we can weaken the creatures!"

Lucifer nodded, his eyes narrowing on Revenor. "Then let's end this."

The three of them charged toward Revenor, their combined power cutting through the shadow creatures that tried to block their path. As they reached him, Revenor unleashed a wave of dark magic that sent them sprawling to the ground.

"Fools," Revenor hissed. "You cannot defeat the Dark Council. Your resistance is futile."

But as Revenor prepared to strike the final blow, a blinding light erupted from Valyron's staff. The light pierced through the darkness, forcing Revenor to recoil in pain. Taking advantage of the moment, Leo leaped forward, his sword blazing with elemental energy, and struck Revenor across the chest.

Revenor staggered back, clutching his wound, his eyes wide with disbelief. "This... cannot be..."

Lucifer stepped forward, his voice cold and determined. "Your darkness is not eternal. It can be defeated."

With a final surge of power, Valyron and Leo combined their magic and strength, unleashing a devastating attack that shattered Revenor's connection to the dark forces. The shadow creatures around them dissolved into mist, and the tendrils retreated into the ground.

Revenor fell to his knees, his strength fading. "You may have won this battle," he gasped, "but the Dark Council will not stop. They will come for you... and they will not show mercy."

Lucifer stood over Revenor, his expression unreadable. "Let them come. We will be ready."

With those final words, Revenor's body disintegrated into dust, carried away by the wind. The camp was silent once more, save for the laboured breathing of the survivors.

Leo sheathed his sword, his shoulders sagging with exhaustion. "That was... too close."

Valyron nodded, wiping the sweat from his brow. "We've bought ourselves some time, but the real battle is still ahead."

Lucifer stared into the distance, his mind already focused on the challenges yet to come. "We'll need to strengthen our forces. This was just a taste of the Dark Council's power. We can't afford to be caught off guard again."

As the night deepened, the three of them stood together, united by the battle they had fought and the battles yet to come. The Dark Council was far from defeated, but for now, they had survived. And in the darkness, they found a spark of hope.

14

THE VEIL OF DECEPTION

The chamber was dimly lit, shadows dancing on the ancient stone walls. The air was thick with the tension of impending treachery. Seated around a circular table, the members of the Dark Council watched Seraphine with cold, calculating eyes.

"You know what is required of you, Seraphine," spoke the leader of the Council, his voice a low growl that echoed in the silence. His gaunt face, hidden beneath a hood, betrayed no emotion, only a gleaming hunger for power. "Lucifer must be weakened. His influence must fade."

Seraphine, her eyes glinting with a cruel determination, nodded slowly. "I will infiltrate his trust. He has always harboured some sentiment toward me. That will be our opening."

The youngest member of the Council, a wiry figure with sharp, bird-like features, leaned forward. "Once you are close, you must gradually poison him. Not in body, but in spirit. Use your abilities to draw out the darkness from within him. Slowly, imperceptibly, so that even he cannot detect it until it is too late."

Seraphine smiled, her lips curling upward in a sly grin. "Leave it to me. Lucifer will never see it coming."

The leader raised a hand to silence the room. "We are counting on you, Seraphine. This is our chance to bring him to his knees. Do not fail us."

With a graceful nod, Seraphine turned and left the chamber, the weight of her mission pressing heavily on her. She knew that the fate of the Dark Council rested on her success. But she was confident—Lucifer's trust in her would be his undoing.

Weeks passed, and Seraphine's presence in Lucifer's court became a familiar sight. She played her part well, offering counsel, friendship, and subtle comfort in moments of doubt. Her proximity allowed her to influence him subtly, her powers working to cloud his judgment and sap his strength.

Lucifer, distracted by the weight of his responsibilities, did not notice the slow change within him. His power waned, but he attributed it to the stress of war, to the countless battles and the looming threat of the Dark Lords. Seraphine, always at his side, offered quiet reassurances, her words laced with venom that poisoned his mind.

Yet, Leo and Valyron began to sense something was wrong. They saw the weariness in Lucifer's eyes, the way he moved with less vigour, how his decisions became clouded. Seraphine's influence was growing too strong, and they could no longer ignore the possibility of treachery.

In the grand hall, Leo and Valyron stood before Lucifer, their expressions grave. Seraphine was absent from this confrontation, her presence elsewhere in the castle.

"Lucifer, we have reason to believe that Seraphine has been manipulating you," Valyron began cautiously. "Your power is fading, and we think she's behind it."

Lucifer frowned, his brow furrowing with confusion. "Seraphine? She has been nothing but loyal to me."

"She may appear that way," Leo interjected, his tone firm. "But we have our suspicions. Her influence over you... it isn't natural."

Lucifer looked between the two of them, doubt flickering in his eyes. "You are suggesting that she has been poisoning me? In spirit?"

"Yes," Valyron replied softly. "We don't think it's a coincidence that you've grown weaker since she arrived. We need to act before it's too late."

For a moment, Lucifer remained silent, the weight of their words sinking in. Then, with a heavy sigh, he nodded. "Very well. If what you say is true, then she must be removed from the castle."

Seraphine's expulsion was swift. She offered no resistance, though her eyes betrayed a hint of satisfaction. As she was led away, she cast one final glance at Lucifer, a knowing smile on her lips. The damage had already been done.

In the depths of the Dark Council's lair, the members gathered once again, their faces alight with cruel satisfaction.

"The plan is working," the leader murmured, his voice a hiss of triumph. "Lucifer grows weaker by the day. Even though Seraphine has been discovered, the seeds of darkness have already been planted."

Another member chuckled darkly. "Soon, he will be too weak to stand against us. And when the time comes, we will strike."

The leader raised his hand, silencing the room once more. "Patience. Let the poison do its work. We will wait until Lucifer is at his weakest before we make our move."

With that, the Council fell into a quiet, sinister anticipation, their eyes gleaming with the promise of victory.

Meanwhile, back in the castle, Valyron struggled with a vision that had haunted him in his sleep. He saw the dark lords advancing upon them, a fierce battle raging in the heart of the kingdom. Amidst the chaos, he saw Lucifer fall, his body crumbling under the weight of his injuries and the darkness that still clung to him.

The vision left Valyron shaken, his mind racing with the fear of what was to come. He knew they had to act quickly, to protect Lucifer before the dark lords launched their final assault.

But how could he reveal the truth to Lucifer without breaking him further? How could he bear the weight of knowing what was to come, without losing hope himself?

Valyron resolved to protect Lucifer at all costs. But he kept the darkest part of his vision to himself, determined to find a way to alter their fate. As Lucifer passed by, he saw Valyron's stressed face. He asked him," What happened Valyron, why are you so sad?" Valyron looked at him, thinking that it would be better to be transparent. "I saw a vision a few days ago, when Seraphine was here. A vision that left me shaken. I.... I saw a battle... against the Dark Council. And... And... I saw that we lost. Not only the battle... but... but... You as well." Lucifer was shocked hearing about it. Nevertheless, he replied, "Valyron, I am not scared of death. If I die fighting the Dark Lords, so be it." As he said these inspirational words, he fell down. With barely a heartbeat and pulse, it seemed Lucifer was going to die.

And so, preparations began for a sacred ritual, far from the castle, that would shield Lucifer from further harm. Lucifer started getting better, but was still in a frail state. However, Valyron trusted the process. After a few hours, Lucifer woke up with anger running through his veins. His body was not strong enough but his mental strength was strong enough for him to believe that he could fight. Leo took charge of the kingdom's defence, rallying the armies and preparing for the battle that loomed on the horizon.

But as the war drums echoed in the distance, Valyron could not shake the fear that they were fighting against a future that had already been written in blood.

The fate of their kingdom, and of Lucifer himself, now hung in the balance.

15

THE LAST STAND

The castle's halls echoed with the heavy tread of boots and whispered prayers as the army prepared for battle. Outside, the distant sound of war drums signalled the Dark Lords' approach. The air was thick with tension, and every soul in the castle knew that this would be their defining moment.

At the war table, Leo stood with his hands braced against the edges, his sharp gaze fixed on the maps. Around him, Valyron, Kael, and the commanders studied the intricate web of defences they had erected.

"The Dark Lords are advancing faster than we anticipated," Leo said, his voice steady but carrying the weight of urgency. "They'll breach our outer defences by nightfall. We need to hold them at the second gate and force them into the bottleneck."

Kael nodded, his battle-worn face grim. "The men are ready. We've reinforced the walls with everything we have. But if they unleash their full power…"

Valyron interrupted, his staff glowing faintly with protective runes. "They will unleash their full power, Kael. That's why we must be relentless."

Lucifer's absence hung over the room like a shadow. Valyron's thoughts lingered on the prophecy, on the vision of Lucifer's death that haunted him. But he shoved it aside. There was no room for doubt now.

As the sun dipped below the horizon, the first clash began. The Dark Lords' army surged forward like a tide of darkness, their ranks a terrifying blend of shadowy creatures and monstrous soldiers. The castle's archers lost volleys of arrows, their fiery tips streaking across the twilight sky and plunging into the oncoming horde. Screams erupted as the flames found their marks, but the enemy's momentum didn't falter.

The Fate of the Fallen

Leo led the charge at the second gate, his sword gleaming as it cut through the first wave of attackers. Beside him, Kael's strikes were precise and brutal, a testament to his years of experience. Valyron stood atop the battlements, weaving spells that created barriers of shimmering light. Each time the enemy's dark magic struck, the barriers rippled but held firm.

For a moment, hope flickered. But then the ground began to tremble. From the heart of the enemy ranks, the Dark Lords themselves emerged. Clad in obsidian armour that seemed to drink the light, their mere presence sent waves of dread rippling through the defenders.

"Hold the line!" Leo shouted, his voice cutting through the chaos. "Do not let them breach the gate!"

The Dark Lords raised their hands, and the sky itself seemed to darken. Bolts of shadow magic tore through the air, shattering stone and throwing soldiers aside like rag dolls. Valyron countered with blasts of energy, but the strain was evident on his face.

Just as the battle seemed to tip in the Dark Lords' favour, a deafening roar split the air. From the castle's keep, Lucifer emerged, astride Draco. Though weakened, his presence was a rallying cry. Soldiers cheered as the dragon soared overhead, breathing torrents of fire that incinerated swathes of the enemy.

Lucifer descended into the fray, his sword drawn, his strikes precise and deadly. But his movements lacked their usual fluidity, a testament to his waning strength. Valyron's heart clenched as he watched, but there was no time to dwell on it. The enemy pressed harder, and the defences were beginning to crumble.

And then, the battlefield shifted. A sudden, chilling laugh echoed through the chaos. From the shadows, Seraphine emerged, her dark robes billowing as if alive. Her eyes glowed with an unnatural light, and the air around her seemed to crackle with malevolence.

"Lucifer," she purred, her voice dripping with mockery. "How noble of you to join us. But tell me, how long can you keep this charade up?"

The Last Stand

Lucifer turned to face her, his grip tightening on his sword. "Seraphine. I should have ended you when I had the chance."

She laughed again, raising her hands. Dark tendrils of magic lashed out, striking Lucifer with force. He staggered but held his ground, retaliating with a surge of light that illuminated the battlefield. The two clashed, their magic colliding in a dazzling display of power that sent shockwaves through the air.

Valyron and Leo fought to hold the line, but the intensity of Lucifer's battle with Seraphine drew their attention. Seraphine's spells were relentless, each one more devastating than the last. She conjured storms of shadow, bolts of lightning that crackled with dark energy. Lucifer countered, his movements a blur despite his injuries. But with every strike, it was clear he was weakening.

"Lucifer!" Valyron shouted, his voice filled with desperation. He cast a protective barrier just in time to deflect a blast aimed at Lucifer's back.

Seraphine's eyes narrowed. "Ah, the ever-loyal Valyron. Tell me, how does it feel to watch your hero fall?"

Before Valyron could respond, she unleashed a massive wave of energy. The barrier shattered, throwing Valyron to the ground. Lucifer roared, his own power surging as he struck back with a spell that momentarily forced her to retreat.

Amid the chaos, the portal ritual was nearing completion. Valyron, battered but determined, dragged himself to the circle he had prepared. The words of the incantation flowed from his lips, the air around him shimmering as the portal began to take shape.

Leo and Kael rallied the remaining soldiers, pushing back the enemy as best they could. But the Dark Lords were relentless, their power seemingly endless. Just as the portal stabilized, Seraphine turned her attention to Valyron.

"You think you can escape?" she hissed, hurling a bolt of shadow at him.

Lucifer intercepted it, the force of the impact driving him to one knee. He looked at Valyron, his eyes blazing. "Finish it!"

With a final surge of strength, Valyron completed the ritual. The portal opened, a swirling vortex of light and shadow. Without hesitation, Leo, Kael, and the elite soldiers charged through, their shouts of determination echoing as they vanished into the Nether.

Lucifer turned back to Seraphine. "Your time ends here."

She smiled coldly. "Let's see if you can make good on that promise."

Their battle reached its climax, the clash of their powers illuminating the darkened battlefield. But even as they fought, the tides were shifting. Valyron, now in the Nether, unleashed his most powerful spell yet. A beam of pure light shot from his staff, piercing through the walls of the Dark Lords' fortress and striking at its heart.

The light spread, consuming the darkness. Seraphine's scream echoed as she was engulfed, her form disintegrating into nothingness. The Dark Lords fell one by one, their power severed as the source of their strength was obliterated.

The fortress crumbled, the ground beneath them shaking as the Nether began to collapse. Valyron, Leo, and Kael barely made it back through the portal before it closed behind them.

On the battlefield, silence fell. The Dark Lords' army, now leaderless, dissolved into shadows. Lucifer stood amidst the ruins, his body battered, his strength nearly gone. But he was alive. And they had won.

Valyron and Leo approached him, their faces etched with a mixture of relief and sorrow. "It's over," Valyron said softly.

Lucifer nodded, his gaze distant. "For now."

The battle had been won, but the cost had been high. As they looked out over the battlefield, the weight of their victory settled on them. They had prevailed, but the scars of the war would remain forever.

16

BREAKING THE VEIL

*T*he echoes of the war still hung in the air as the morning light pierced through the castle windows. Outside, the remains of a brutal battle lay scattered—broken weapons, shattered shields, and the blood of fallen warriors. Inside the castle walls, however, was an even more fragile sight: the champions of this fight, now worn down, weary, and facing challenges that were not so easily conquered.

Lucifer sat alone in his chambers, his dark eyes fixed on the shadows dancing across the floor. His body was still recovering from Seraphine's intoxicating influence, but the real wound was deeper. The war had left him victorious, but with each passing day, he felt the pull of darkness within him growing stronger. The powers he once used to command now seemed to demand more than he was willing to give.

"I thought this was behind me," he whispered, his voice barely audible. "But the darkness… it never truly leaves."

Valyron entered quietly, sensing the weight of Lucifer's thoughts. "You did what you had to," he said, though his own voice carried the tremor of uncertainty.

Lucifer looked up, his pride battling against the vulnerability that he despised so much. "What if this darkness… consumes me? What if I become what I once fought against?"

Valyron remained silent for a moment, choosing his words carefully. "Then we'll fight it together. We've faced worse and prevailed."

But even as Valyron spoke, doubt gnawed at him. He had been pushing his magic to the limits, drawing on every spell, every ounce of power he had, and still, it never seemed to be enough. His parents had left him with a legacy of greatness, but now, standing in the aftermath of the battle, he wondered if he could ever live up to their expectations.

"I should have been stronger," Valyron admitted, surprising even himself with the confession. "If I had mastered more spells, perfected my craft... perhaps we wouldn't have come so close to defeat."

Lucifer looked at him sharply, recognizing the same self-doubt that he had been grappling with. "Perfection doesn't win wars, Valyron. Grit does. And you've shown more than enough of that."

Yet, even as Lucifer tried to reassure his ally, his own words felt hollow. He was their leader, their king, but how could he continue to lead when he himself was falling apart?

Meanwhile, Leo stood outside, surveying the remnants of the battlefield. The weight of leadership had always rested heavily on his shoulders, but after this fight, it seemed to crush him. For all his strength, for all his skill, there had been moments when he had doubted whether he could protect those he cared about. In the heat of battle, he had charged forward recklessly, driven by a need to prove himself. And in doing so, he had nearly cost them everything.

Apex approached, his massive frame casting a shadow across Leo. "You fought well," Apex said simply.

Leo didn't respond at first, his gaze fixed on the horizon. "I was reckless," he finally admitted. "I could've gotten us all killed."

Apex frowned, not accustomed to hearing such self-criticism from Leo. "You did what needed to be done."

"But did I?" Leo snapped, his frustration boiling over. "I rushed in, thinking I could take on the world. What if next time, I'm not so lucky? What if I lead us all to ruin?"

Apex remained silent for a moment, considering his words carefully. "We all have our demons, Leo. I fight mine every day, but you can't let them control you. You need to find balance."

Leo's jaw tightened, but he nodded. He knew Apex was right, but the path to balance seemed more elusive than ever.

Later that evening, as the fire crackled in the grand hall, the group gathered to reflect on their victory. But the mood was far from celebratory.

"Lucifer," Leo began cautiously, "what's next? We can't keep fighting like this forever."

Lucifer glanced at him, a shadow of his former self. "I don't know," he confessed. "I thought defeating the Dark Lords would bring peace, but all I feel is... emptiness. And this darkness inside me... it's growing stronger."

Valyron placed a hand on Lucifer's shoulder. "We're with you, no matter what happens."

Lucifer looked at his friends, the people who had fought by his side, and felt a pang of guilt. They deserved better than a leader who was slowly unravelling. But for now, all he could do was nod and hope that, together, they could find a way forward.

That night, as the castle settled into an uneasy quiet, Valyron tossed and turned in his sleep. In his dreams, he saw a vision—a vision of another war, fiercer than the last. And this time, he saw them losing. He saw Lucifer falling, consumed by the darkness that was slowly overtaking him. He saw their kingdom in flames, their hopes reduced to ashes.

Valyron woke with a start, his heart pounding in his chest. He couldn't let this vision come to pass. But how could he stop it without revealing to Lucifer the fate that awaited him?

For now, all he could do was keep this terrible secret and hope that they could find a way to change the future. The burden of his vision weighed heavily on him, but Valyron knew that revealing it might only hasten the very doom he had seen.

Outside, the wind howled through the night, carrying with it the whispers of battles yet to come.

17

SHADOWS OF DESTINY

Lucifer stared at the growing number of refugees pouring into his kingdom, their faces hollowed by fear and exhaustion. He had seen this before, time and again—villagers fleeing the cruelty of rulers who valued power over their people. Yet, each new face seemed to tear at his soul, a stark reminder of the darkness that continued to corrupt the world.

"Apex," he called softly, trying to keep his voice steady. Apex stood at the edge of the crowd, his eyes fixed on a group of haggard villagers who had just arrived. There was something in his expression, something deeper than just concern for strangers.

Apex's gaze didn't waver. His hands clenched into fists at his sides. "They're from my village," he said through gritted teeth, his voice barely above a whisper. "Those people… they're my family."

Lucifer frowned, stepping closer. "Your family? Apex, what happened?"

Apex's breathing quickened, and his voice trembled with anger. "That wretch of a man… he was nothing but a greedy, power-hungry fool. He overthrew our rightful king and turned our home into a living nightmare. My parents—" Apex's voice broke for a moment, but he swallowed hard, pushing the emotion down. "My parents were supposed to be safe. I sent them away so they wouldn't suffer like the rest of us. But now…"

He turned to Lucifer, his eyes burning with a mix of fury and desperation. "This can't continue. We can't just let this happen. We need to do something! I need to stop him before he destroys everything I care about."

Lucifer placed a hand on Apex's shoulder, his own heart heavy with empathy. "Apex, I understand your pain. I've faced those who've taken everything from me, too. But rushing into this won't bring justice—it'll only bring more bloodshed. We need a plan."

Apex shook his head fiercely. "No! I can't wait anymore. I've already lost so much. My people—my family—need me now! I won't let that tyrant continue to ruin their lives. We have to act, Lucifer. We have to stop him!"

Lucifer's eyes darkened. He could feel Apex's rage and sorrow radiating off him, like heat from a wildfire. He remembered his own fury, his own need for vengeance against those who had wronged him. But he also knew the consequences of acting blindly, of letting anger take control.

He sighed, keeping his voice calm but firm. "We will act, Apex. But not recklessly. We'll take back your village, but we must do it strategically. We need to be smart, or we'll end up like every other resistance that's fallen to the greed of tyrants."

Apex's jaw tightened, his breath heavy with frustration. "I just... I can't stand it anymore, Lucifer. I can't stand seeing them suffer like this. I feel so helpless."

Lucifer's hand remained steady on Apex's shoulder, grounding him. "You're not helpless, Apex. You're strong, and that strength can save them. But only if you use it wisely. We'll stop that selfish king, together. But first, we prepare. You've seen what haste and anger can do. We can't let that be our downfall."

Apex looked into Lucifer's eyes, the fury slowly cooling, replaced by something steadier—determination. He nodded, albeit reluctantly. "Fine. But promise me this: we don't wait too long. I don't want my parents or my people to suffer for another moment longer."

Lucifer nodded. "I promise, Apex. We'll move quickly, but we'll move smartly. And when the time comes, we'll make sure that tyrant pays for what he's done."

Apex exhaled deeply, the tension in his shoulders easing slightly. "Thank you, Lucifer. I won't let you down."

As they turned back toward the castle, Lucifer's mind raced. He could feel the weight of leadership pressing on him again, the responsibility to protect not only his own kingdom but also the people Apex had sworn to save. But this time, he would not do it alone. Together, they would bring justice to a world that had seen too little of it.

And they would do it on their terms.

18

THE REBIRTH OF THE KING

The aftermath of the war with the Dark Lords left a haunting silence in the once-vibrant kingdom. The bodies of fallen enemies and allies alike had been cleared from the battlefield, and the heavy fog of destruction was beginning to lift. But the true battle was not over yet, at least not for Lucifer.

Despite the victorious cries of his people and the celebration of freedom across the lands, Lucifer could feel the lingering weight of the dark magic that had once threatened to consume him. He had fought through the pain, the weakness seeping into his bones from Seraphine's treachery. He had fought because his people needed him, because abandoning them in their hour of need was unthinkable. And with Apex gone, planning for revenge.... planning to set his village free, the load to handle the kingdom was also more.

Now, with the Dark Lords gone, Lucifer was the one in need of healing.

The king sat on the balcony of his chamber, staring out at the horizon. The land that once carried the scars of battle was beginning to heal, much like the people who had been saved. Villagers returned to their homes, their faces filled with cautious hope, but Lucifer's mind was far from the bustling life below.

The door creaked open, and Leo entered, his expression concerned as he approached Lucifer. "You should be resting," Leo said, his voice steady but gentle. "You've barely had time to recover from the final battle."

Lucifer, still pale and visibly weakened, offered a faint smile. "Resting… is not so easy when the weight of the crown never leaves your head."

Leo stood beside him, gazing out at the kingdom. "We won. The Dark Lords are no more. You gave everything in that fight, even when you were nearly destroyed. But now you have to take care of yourself."

Lucifer sighed, rubbing his chest, the place where Seraphine's dark influence had burrowed deep. Even though she was long gone, the effects of her poisonous touch still lingered.

"Seraphine's treachery... the war... it feels like it's still with me," Lucifer admitted, his voice heavy. "I fought through it because I had to. But now that the battle's over, I can feel it eating away at me. I'm not sure how much longer I can go on like this."

Leo knelt beside him, his tone serious but compassionate. "That's why Valyron and I called Kael. We need his help to heal you completely. You may have purged most of the dark magic from your body, but some of it still remains."

Lucifer's brow furrowed. "Kael? I thought he'd gone into hiding after the war."

"He did," Leo replied, "but he's agreed to help. He knows how important it is that you recover fully. The kingdom can't afford to lose you now."

At that moment, Valyron entered the room, his expression grim yet determined. "Kael has agreed to meet us in the sacred grove. We need to perform the final ritual to cleanse the remnants of Seraphine's influence."

Lucifer looked between his two closest allies, the weight of their words sinking in. His people needed a strong leader now more than ever, but the darkness inside him was slowly draining his strength.

"I can't leave the kingdom again," Lucifer said, his voice raw. "They've just begun to rebuild. What will they think if their king vanishes so soon after victory?"

Valyron shook his head. "Lucifer, if you don't heal, there won't be a kingdom left to lead. The damage Seraphine did will kill you if we don't act now."

Lucifer hesitated, his gaze drifting back to the kingdom below. His people had already suffered so much—could he really afford to leave them again, even if it was for his own sake?

Leo placed a hand on his shoulder. "We'll handle things here. I'll take charge in your absence. Valyron and I have planned for this. You just need to trust us."

Lucifer closed his eyes, the exhaustion creeping back into his bones. Trust. It was something he had always struggled with, especially after Seraphine's betrayal. But looking at Leo and Valyron, the two who had fought by his side through everything, he knew they were right.

"Fine," Lucifer finally relented. "But if anything happens to the kingdom in my absence, I'll never forgive myself."

Valyron nodded, satisfied with Lucifer's decision. "We'll leave at dawn. The sooner we begin the ritual, the sooner you'll be restored."

As the conversation continued, a shadow loomed over them. Unseen by anyone in the room, a dark presence stirred, watching and waiting. Though the Dark Lords had been defeated, something far older, far more dangerous, had taken notice of the weakened king.

In the deepest corners of the Nether, Kharon stirred.

The ritual began at sunrise, in the sacred grove far from the heart of the kingdom. Kael, the mysterious healer and ally, stood by, guiding the ancient magic that would cleanse Lucifer fully. He and Leo watched from the side, their weapons sheathed but ready, just in case the ritual attracted unwanted attention while Valyron was performing the ritual.

As Valyron chanted, the air thickened with power. A swirling vortex of light formed around Lucifer, lifting him off the ground as the ritual took hold. The remnants of Seraphine's dark magic pulsed through him, resisting the cleansing force, but Valyron's magic was strong.

"Stay with us, Lucifer," Valyron's voice echoed through the grove as the light intensified. "You must fight it. The last remains of darkness are clinging to your soul."

Lucifer gritted his teeth, feeling the familiar grip of Seraphine's influence tightening around his chest. But this time, instead of giving in, he pushed back. He could feel the light Kael had summoned, feel the strength returning to his limbs. The poison that had plagued him for so long began to dissolve, piece by piece, until finally, it was gone.

When the light faded, Lucifer collapsed to the ground, gasping for breath. The silence in the grove was deafening as everyone waited to see if the ritual had worked.

Slowly, Lucifer stood, his body weak but no longer weighed down by darkness. He looked at Kael, Leo, and Valyron, a spark of hope in his eyes.

"It's over," Kael said quietly. "You're free."

Lucifer took a deep breath, feeling the air fill his lungs without pain for the first time in what felt like an eternity. He nodded, a small, relieved smile playing on his lips. "Thank you… all of you."

But just as the weight of relief settled over them, a chill ran through the grove. Valyron stiffened, his eyes narrowing as he sensed something wrong. Leo instinctively reached for his weapon, scanning the trees for any sign of danger.

Kael was the first to speak. "We need to leave. Now."

Lucifer looked at him, confused. "What's wrong?"

Kael's face was pale, his voice low and urgent. "There's something else… something far worse than the Dark Lords."

In the distance, the wind began to howl, carrying with it a whisper, a name.

Kharon!

19

TIME FOR RECLAMATION

Apex stood near the village square, the faces of his fellow villagers filled with despair. The memories of his past flooded his mind, every corner of this place reminding him of the life he once had before the selfish king took over. Now, the village was nothing more than a shadow of its former self, crushed under the weight of greed. The sight of the downtrodden citizens fuelled a fire in Apex's heart—a fire he was determined to set ablaze.

He had to take action, and he had to do it now.

That evening, sitting at the modest table in the village inn, Apex began drafting his plan. His fingers ran over the worn edges of a map spread across the table, his mind already visualizing the different paths and strategies that could be used in the fight. He looked at the villages surrounding his home, the ones that had yet to fall under the tyrant's control.

"If we can convince them to join our cause, we stand a chance," Apex muttered to himself.

But it wasn't just about convincing others—it was about reigniting the spark of rebellion within his people. Apex knew that the villagers had lost hope, that years of oppression had crushed their spirits. He had to show them there was still something worth fighting for.

He stood and addressed the group gathered in the inn—his friends, neighbours, and those who had once known him as the boy who had left, only to return as a soldier. "The king has taken everything from us—our land, our freedom, our dignity. But what he cannot take is our will to fight back."

Eyes widened as they looked at Apex. A few muttered in disbelief. But Apex continued, his voice strong and determined. "I've seen what we can do when we come together. I've seen us thrive before the greed of one man tore us apart. Now is the time to reclaim what's ours!"

A few older men exchanged glances. One of them, a blacksmith, stood and cleared his throat. "What you're asking isn't easy, lad. We've lived under his rule for years. We're not fighters anymore. We're broken."

Apex took a deep breath. He knew their fear, he had seen it time and time again, but this was different. They were fighting for their homes. "We don't need an army of soldiers—we need people who care enough to defend their families, their homes. I'll train you. We have weapons, and I know how to use them. If you can wield a hammer, you can fight. If you can tend to a farm, you can protect it."

The room fell silent. Slowly, one by one, people began to nod. Apex's words carried the conviction they had lost. The fire in his eyes, the determination in his voice—it was contagious.

"Tomorrow," Apex announced, "we gather all able men and women. We'll teach them how to fight, how to defend themselves, how to plan and strike when the time comes. But first, we need to spread the word to the neighbouring villages."

A man in the corner raised his hand. "How do you plan to do that without alerting the king's spies?"

Apex smirked. "We don't. We want the king to know something is brewing, but not enough to know what. He'll be on edge, but by the time he realizes what's happening, it'll be too late."

His plan was clear. They would move under the guise of gathering resources, holding town meetings, pretending to talk about mundane matters, while secretly rallying support from the surrounding villages. The king's spies might suspect something, but they wouldn't know the full extent of the rebellion until it was too late.

Over the next few days, the village square became a training ground. Men and women who had once been farmers, bakers, and merchants now stood side by side, practicing with makeshift weapons. Apex led the training sessions, his voice steady and encouraging, his actions precise and deliberate.

He showed them how to move in unison, how to wield whatever they had as a weapon—axes, pitchforks, even simple wooden clubs. But more than that, he taught them how to think like soldiers. "You don't have to be stronger than the king's men, but you have to be smarter. We fight with our hearts, not just our hands."

Every night, Apex would gather with his closest allies to review their progress and tweak their strategy. His thoughts constantly returned to the selfish king who now sat comfortably in the castle, believing his rule was unshakable. Apex would prove him wrong.

One night, while sitting with a small group of trusted villagers, Apex outlined the final phase of his plan. "Once we've gathered enough support and trained the villagers, we'll send word to the king. We'll demand he surrender."

"Do you think he'll actually listen?" one of the villagers asked.

"No," Apex replied, "but it'll force him to make the first move. When he sends his forces, they'll be walking into a trap. We'll be ready for them."

The villagers looked at each other, fear mixing with a new sense of hope. They had a leader now. Someone who believed in them. Someone who was willing to fight for them.

A few days later, as the village buzzed with preparations, Apex stood on the hill overlooking his home. The sun was setting, casting long shadows across the land. His thoughts drifted to his parents, who had suffered under the rule of the greedy king. He clenched his fists, the anger rising in his chest. This fight wasn't just for the village—it was personal.

As the wind whispered through the trees, Apex made a vow to himself. He would not rest until his village was free, until the greedy king was dethroned, and until justice had been served. Not until Drenek was overthrown.

In the days that followed, Apex's plan continued to unfold. Messages were sent to nearby villages, and support for the rebellion grew. More people arrived, ready to join the fight. The village was alive with the sounds of training, the clang of weapons being forged, and the whispers of hope.

As the final preparations were made, Apex stood before the gathered villagers once more. "This is our time," he said, his voice carrying across the square. "This is our moment to take back what was stolen from us. We fight not for glory, but for our homes, for our families, for the future we deserve."

The crowd erupted in cheers, their fear replaced by determination. Apex looked out at them, proud of what they had become. They were no longer the broken people he had returned to. They were fighters, ready to reclaim their land.

20

THE WAGING WAR

The village lay before them, quiet in the pale light of early morning. But there was something in the air—an electricity that hummed in Apex's veins. Today was the day everything would change. He stood at the head of his ragtag army, watching the slow smoke rising from the village. He had also called Kael for help. The time for planning was over. It was time for action.

"Remember," Apex began, his voice firm but low, "we are not just fighting for revenge. We're fighting for our future. For our homes, our families." His eyes swept over the small group of fighters—farmers, blacksmiths, villagers who had never held a weapon in their lives until now. "This is our only chance. We win today, or we lose everything."

There was a ripple of murmured agreement. The tension was thick in the air, each man and woman clutching their makeshift weapons a little tighter. Apex's heart pounded, but he kept his expression steady. They looked up to him now—he was the one leading them back to their home, back to the place Drenek had stolen.

Kael, his most trusted fighter, stepped up beside him. "The scouts are in position. As soon as we strike, they'll block the exits. No one leaves unless we want them to."

Apex gave a sharp nod. "Good. Let's make sure Drenek gets that message."

The sun had barely crept over the horizon when the first attack hit. Apex and his team moved with practiced silence, slipping through the narrow streets of the village. The arsenal was their first target. If they could seize the weapons, they'd stand a better chance when it came to facing Drenek's trained soldiers.

Apex signalled with a raised hand, and the group split off, surrounding the arsenal. The guards were lazing at their posts, unaware of the danger creeping towards them. With a swift, silent motion, Kael led the charge, overpowering the guards before they had a chance to sound the alarm. Apex watched as his people worked with the precision of a well-oiled machine, overtaking the arsenal with ruthless efficiency.

As soon as the doors were breached, Apex rushed inside, scanning the rows of weapons. Swords, axes, shields—everything they would need to stand a chance against Drenek's forces. He turned to the group behind him. "Arm yourselves quickly. We move to the palace next."

With the arsenal under their control, Apex's group moved toward the palace. The streets were eerily quiet, the village still waking from its slumber. But soon enough, the alarm would spread. They needed to strike before Drenek's soldiers could organize themselves.

The palace gates loomed ahead, guarded by several soldiers dressed in armour, their expressions hard and unyielding. Apex's heart thudded in his chest. This was it. The moment of truth.

"We go on my mark," Apex whispered to Kael. "Take them out fast and hard."

Kael nodded, and within seconds, the group launched their attack. Apex led the charge, his sword flashing in the morning light as it clashed against the first guard's spear. The sound of battle erupted around him—shouts, the clang of steel, the thud of bodies hitting the ground.

Apex fought with precision, his movements sharp and decisive. But these soldiers were more skilled than the armed guards, and they fought fiercely to defend the palace. Apex felt his muscles burning, sweat pouring down his back as he cut down one opponent after another.

Finally, after what felt like hours, the gates fell. Apex wiped the blood from his blade and motioned for his group to follow. "We don't stop until we've taken the throne room."

Inside the palace, the atmosphere was oppressive. High ceilings loomed above them, and the once opulent hallways were now filled with the stench of fear.

Apex's group moved with urgency, taking down any guards they encountered along the way.

At the doors of the throne room, Apex paused. This was it. Drenek would be inside, waiting for him. He glanced at Kael, who gave a quick nod of encouragement, and then, without hesitation, he pushed the doors open.

The throne room was dark, lit only by the flickering of torches on the walls. Drenek sat on his throne at the far end of the room, his figure shrouded in shadow. He didn't rise to greet Apex as the boy entered, but his eyes gleamed with cold amusement.

"So, the boy returns to face his death," Drenek sneered, his voice dripping with arrogance.

Apex felt a surge of anger flare in his chest, but he kept his expression calm. He stepped forward, his sword held steady at his side. "This ends today, Drenek. Your reign is over."

Drenek chuckled, rising from his throne with slow, deliberate movements. His fingers trailed along the armrests as he stood, his eyes locked on Apex's. "You think you can defeat me?" he said, his voice mocking. "You and your little band of peasants?"

Apex met his gaze with unwavering determination. "We already have. The village is ours again. And soon, this palace will be too."

Drenek's eyes narrowed. "You're a fool, boy. I made this village what it is. Without me, it would've been forgotten, left to rot like the others. I am the reason this land survives!"

Apex took another step forward, his sword now raised. "You're the reason it suffers."

The air in the room crackled with tension. Apex knew Drenek wouldn't go down without a fight. He could see it in the man's eyes—the flicker of desperation, the thinly veiled fear that lingered just beneath his smug facade.

Then, without warning, Drenek lunged.

The attack was sudden, but Apex had been ready for it. Drenek moved fast, but not fast enough. Apex parried the blow, their swords clashing with a deafening ring that echoed through the throne room.

The battle between them was fierce, each strike filled with the weight of years of hatred and betrayal. Drenek fought with the desperation of a man who knew his time was running out, but Apex fought with something stronger—hope.

"You think you can take everything from me?" Drenek snarled, his sword swinging wildly. "I built this village! I am its king!"

Apex gritted his teeth, parrying another blow. "You built nothing but your own ego. You destroyed lives for your greed."

The clash of steel rang out again, and for a moment, they were locked in a deadly dance, neither gaining the upper hand. But Apex was younger, faster. He could feel Drenek's movements slowing, his strikes becoming more erratic.

"You should've stayed away, boy," Drenek spat, his breath laboured. "This village belongs to me!"

Apex's face hardened as he shoved Drenek back, their blades still locked. "Not anymore."

With a final surge of strength, Apex disarmed Drenek, sending the king's sword clattering across the floor. Drenek stumbled backward, his chest heaving with exhaustion. His face was twisted with rage, but there was fear in his eyes now—real fear.

Apex stood over him, his sword raised. The room was eerily quiet, the battle outside forgotten as the two faced off.

"You think killing me will make you a hero?" Drenek sneered, but there was a tremble in his voice now. "You'll be just like me—a murderer."

Apex hesitated, his grip tightening on the hilt of his sword. He could end it right now, with one swift strike. Drenek deserved it—after everything he had done, after all the lives he had ruined. But something held him back.

"I'm nothing like you," Apex said quietly, lowering his sword. "And I never will be."

Drenek's eyes widened in disbelief. "You... you're sparing me?"

Apex's gaze was cold, unyielding. "I'm giving you a choice. Leave this village and never return. If I ever see your face again, I won't hesitate."

Drenek scrambled to his feet, the shock still etched on his face. He glanced at Apex, then at the door, and without another word, he fled from the throne room.

Apex watched him go, his heart still pounding in his chest. He had won. The village was free.

As Apex stepped out of the palace, the cheers of his people echoed in his ears. They had done it. The village was theirs again.

But as the crowd gathered around him, their faces filled with hope and relief, Apex couldn't help but feel the weight of what was yet to come. This was just the beginning. The battle for their future had only just begun.

21

THE DUAL REIGN

*T*he village was finally theirs, but a strange quiet had settled over the people. Even after the celebrations, the looming question of who would lead them weighed heavily. The palace, stripped of Drenek's cruelty, was now empty of a ruler. The villagers were looking to Apex and Kael—both of them standing at the heart of the main square, surrounded by those who had fought by their sides.

Apex looked up at the crumbling palace, its imposing walls still standing, but hollow inside. He had never imagined himself sitting on the throne that Drenek had once occupied. It didn't feel right. He had fought to reclaim his home, to free the people, not to rule them.

"I think it should be you," Apex said quietly, turning to Kael, who stood beside him, arms crossed as he surveyed the village.

Kael raised an eyebrow. "Me? You're the one who led them to victory. They follow you, Apex."

Apex shook his head. "They followed us, Kael. You were the one who organized the attack, who got the people to rise up. You know this village better than anyone. You've lived here all your life."

Kael's jaw tightened, his eyes darkening. "And so have you. You're Drenek's heir—the rightful ruler. They'll respect you. They'll listen to you because of who you are."

Apex clenched his fists, frustration bubbling to the surface. "I didn't fight to replace Drenek. I don't want to be king!"

The crowd around them murmured quietly, sensing the tension between the two. Apex took a deep breath, trying to steady his thoughts. He knew Kael was right in some ways. The people expected him to take the throne, to lead them. But that wasn't the life he wanted.

"You've been leading them this whole time," Kael continued, his voice firm but not unkind. "You can't just walk away now. They need someone they can trust."

"I trust you," Apex shot back, his voice rising. "You know how to lead. You've been doing it longer than I have."

Kael's eyes flashed with frustration. "And that's exactly why I shouldn't be the one. I'm not fit for the throne. I've been a fighter all my life. I don't know anything about ruling."

"You think I do?" Apex's voice was filled with disbelief. "I'm barely out of my teens! I wouldn't know where to start."

The two stood in silence for a moment, the weight of responsibility pressing down on both of them. Apex could see the strain in Kael's eyes, the reluctance to take on the burden of leadership. But he also knew Kael was right—neither of them felt truly ready for the throne.

Before they could argue further, a voice called out from the crowd.

"What about the old legends?" an elder said, stepping forward from the group of villagers. His voice was raspy, but there was strength in his gaze. "There was a story, once told to us by our ancestors… about the one who would come when we needed them most. A saviour, a ruler from the shadows. Perhaps now is the time."

Kael frowned, turning to the elder. "What are you talking about?"

The old man smiled, though there was something unsettling in his expression. "The legend of Kharon. He was said to have been the rightful king, long before Drenek ever ruled. His bloodline was lost, but the prophecy said he would return one day, in our darkest hour."

Apex felt a chill run down his spine at the mention of the name. He had heard whispers of Kharon before, but they had always been dismissed as myths—stories told to scare children.

"The dark king," Apex muttered under his breath, remembering the tales.

"That's just a story," Kael said, dismissing the elder with a wave of his hand. "We need a leader who's here. Someone we can rely on."

The elder's gaze was piercing as he looked between Apex and Kael. "You may think it's just a story, but stories have a way of becoming real when the time is right."

Apex's mind raced, trying to make sense of the old man's words. Was Kharon truly real? Was he still out there, waiting for the moment to reclaim the throne?

"I've heard rumours," Apex said quietly, glancing at Kael. "Whispers of Kharon's followers, gathering in secret."

Kael's eyes narrowed. "Are you saying you believe this?"

"I don't know," Apex admitted. "But if there's even a chance that Kharon is real, that he's planning to return... we need to be ready."

Kael shook his head. "We can't build our future on legends, Apex. We need to lead, not wait for some mythical figure to come and save us."

Apex could see the frustration in Kael's eyes, but there was something in the elder's words that gnawed at the back of his mind. The village may have been free of Drenek, but there were still dangers lurking in the shadows. If Kharon truly existed, then he could be a greater threat than they ever imagined.

The crowd grew restless as the debate between Apex and Kael continued. Finally, Apex held up a hand, silencing the murmurs.

"We can't afford to wait for someone else to take charge," he said, his voice steady. "But we also can't ignore the possibility that Kharon is real. We need to stay vigilant, to prepare for whatever may come."

Kael nodded slowly, though his expression remained tense. "So, what do we do? Who takes the throne?"

The Dual Reign

Apex hesitated, looking out at the faces of the villagers. They had fought so hard for this moment, for the chance to rebuild their home. He didn't want to let them down.

But he also didn't want to be the one sitting on the throne.

Finally, Apex took a deep breath and turned to Kael. "You lead the council. Together, we'll make decisions for the village. No king, no crown—just a group of people working together to make things right."

Kael's eyes softened, and after a long moment, he nodded. "I can live with that."

The villagers murmured their agreement, and Apex felt a weight lift off his shoulders. It wasn't a perfect solution, but it was the best one they had for now.

But even as the village began to settle into its new way of life, Apex couldn't shake the feeling that Kharon was out there, watching. Waiting.

The legend wasn't over. It was just the beginning.

22

A VILLAIN MADE

The sky above Silent Mountain was a blanket of thick, swirling clouds, casting a shadow over the path as Lucifer, Kael, Apex, Valyron, and Leo marched forward. The summons had come suddenly, a scroll from Lucifer instructing them to travel to the mountain where, according to old rumours, the remaining Dark Lords had retreated. Despite the victory they had achieved, not all of the dark forces had been vanquished.

Apex walked with a determined pace, his thoughts filled with the growing responsibility of his plan to save his home. But now, this new threat loomed over them, and the weight of it was evident in the strained silence between the group.

As they neared the mountain's base, Lucifer stopped abruptly, his eyes narrowing.

"They're here," he said, his voice low but clear. "The Dark Lords weren't completely destroyed. They've been guarding something—something powerful."

Apex exchanged a glance with Kael, the sense of danger thickening with every step.

"What could they possibly be protecting?" Valyron asked, gripping his staff tightly.

"Something ancient," Lucifer replied, his gaze never leaving the path ahead. "A stone—one that holds the power to bring back Kharon."

Leo frowned. "Kharon? But he was—"

"Not fully destroyed," Lucifer interrupted. "They're trying to revive him. And if they succeed, he'll be more powerful than any of us can imagine."

The tension among them grew as they pushed onward. The mountain's eerie stillness contrasted with the storm of thoughts in Apex's mind. The idea of facing Kharon, someone who had once looked up to Lucifer only to be rejected, now twisted by darkness, was unsettling.

They reached the summit after hours of climbing, and there it was—the stone. It sat in the centre of a dark clearing, glowing faintly, pulsing with an otherworldly energy. Surrounding it were the remaining Dark Lords, their figures cloaked in shadows as they chanted in a language lost to time.

Lucifer stepped forward, his voice a command. "Stop this now, or face the end."

The Dark Lords paused, turning slowly to face the intruders. One of them, larger and more menacing than the rest, stepped forward.

"You're too late, Lucifer," the Dark Lord rasped. "Kharon will rise again, and with him, darkness will reign once more." As soon as they started saying some spell to resurrect Kharon, they were struck by Lucifer's sword. Leo and Valyron, together formed deadly attacks. And one by one, the last of the Lords also fell down.

Meanwhile, Kael and Apex's focus was on the stone. There was a hand print on the stone. Maybe that would resurrect Kharon. Apex then spoke," Well, the Dark Lords tried to resurrect him to get a powerful ally on their side. Then, why shouldn't we?" Kael and Leo thought of it as a good idea. However, Valyron and Lucifer were a bit reluctant.

Apex laid his hand on the stone and felt nothing happening. Just then the stone started glowing and cracks were found on the stone. As they moved toward the stone, the ground beneath them began to tremble. Cracks appeared in the earth as well, and the stone glowed brighter, its power reaching its peak.

A loud crack echoed through the air as the stone shattered, releasing a wave of dark energy that knocked them all back. The ground beneath Apex gave way, and before anyone could react, he slipped, falling into the widening chasm.

"Apex!" Kael shouted, rushing toward the edge, but it was too late. The void swallowed Apex whole, his cry fading into the darkness.

Leo, Valyron, and Lucifer scrambled to pull Kael back as the chasm continued to widen. Apex was gone.

The shock of his loss hung in the air as they stood, breathless, staring at the void where their friend had fallen. There was no time to mourn because of what lay ahead. But they all gave them tribute.

As the dust settled, the energy from the stone coalesced into a figure. Kharon stood tall, his eyes glowing with newfound power. He scanned the group, his gaze finally settling on Lucifer.

"Lucifer," Kharon's voice was soft but filled with strength. "I am here, as I always wished. My idol, let me serve you. Let me be part of your court."

Lucifer's face darkened. "You don't understand, Kharon. I can't let you. You've become too dangerous. If you go out of control, the destruction you could cause—"

Kharon's expression shifted from hope to disbelief. "You reject me again? Even now, after everything just happened. Even you know I am more powerful than that young fallen warrior there!"

Lucifer stepped forward. "It's not about rejection, Kharon. It's about the negativity you bring. You have risen again because of the darkness and that darkness now flows inside you. "

Kharon's hands clenched into fists, his body trembling with the weight of Lucifer's words. "If you could do it, why not me? I admired you... I wanted to be like you. And now, you're casting me aside?"

Lucifer said, "This darkness that flows inside you is what gives you the power. I was always oppressing it. My real power comes from the support from my friends, my citizens and the righteousness which I follow."

The air grew thick with tension, and for a moment, it seemed as if Kharon might unleash the very power Lucifer feared. But then he took a step back, his face hardening with resolve.

A Villain Made

"If you won't accept me... then perhaps the world will learn to fear me instead."

With those words, Kharon turned, vanishing into the shadows, leaving behind only the echo of his final threat.

The group stood in silence, mourning the loss of Apex and fearing the future that now lay ahead. The Dark Lords were gone, but Kharon's awakening had set something far worse into motion.

23

THE CALL TO ARMS

*K*haron stood at the edge of the cliff, gazing out over the dark expanse of the valley below. The shadows of the mountains loomed large, mirroring the growing darkness within his heart. Rejected by Lucifer, the idol he had longed to impress, Kharon felt a burning desire for revenge ignite within him. He would no longer remain in the shadows, waiting for recognition. Instead, he would carve his own path and seize the power that had been denied to him.

The memory of Lucifer's dismissive words echoed in his mind, fuelling his fury. He envisioned the kingdom of Lightfall, its golden spires and vibrant banners, now a symbol of everything he loathed. With every heartbeat, Kharon resolved to bring it crashing down. To do that, he needed an army—a formidable force made up of those who had suffered under Lucifer's rule, those who harboured resentment and anger.

Kharon sat at his desk, his quill scratching against the parchment as he crafted a single message meant for multiple recipients. It was a call to arms, an invitation to join him in his quest for vengeance. He addressed the letter to various kings and individuals who had once opposed Lucifer, each of whom had their own grievances against the ruler of Lightfall.

To the Disgraced Rulers and Warriors:

"To all who have suffered under the tyranny of Lucifer,

You know well the pain of loss, the sting of betrayal, and the crushing weight of ambition thwarted. For too long, we have watched as he crushed our hopes and dreams beneath his heel, all while masquerading as a benevolent king.

The Call to Arms

We have endured the humiliation of defeat and the agony of watching our kingdoms crumble.

I, Kharon, am calling upon you to rise against the very man who has wronged us all. Together, we can forge an army that will challenge the might of Lightfall, reclaim what is rightfully ours, and restore honour to our names.

Join me at the Shadowed Vale in three nights. There, we will unite our forces and set our sights on overthrowing the tyrant. Do not let this opportunity pass you by; the time for vengeance is now.

Kharon."

Once the letters were sealed, Kharon summoned his most trusted ravens and sent them off into the night sky, each carrying his message to the intended recipients. He could envision the responses—the flicker of hope igniting in the hearts of those who had long given up.

As Kharon awaited replies, he began plotting the next phase of his plan. He recalled the faces of the rulers and warriors he sought to unite, each with their own motivations for seeking revenge against Lucifer.

King Thessius of Solvanor had once stood as a powerful ruler, his empire vast and prosperous until Lucifer's forces had crushed him, leaving him in disgrace. Kharon believed that if he could rekindle Thessius's desire for power, he could secure a vital ally.

Queen Astrid of the Stormcliff Isles had seen her navy decimated by Lucifer's arrogance. She was known for her fierce spirit and unyielding resolve. Kharon imagined her fury at the thought of retribution, knowing she would be an invaluable asset to his cause.

Kadrin, the Banished Knight, had once fought bravely alongside Lucifer, but his ambition and greed for power, made him thirst for positions. Lucifer having realised his limitations was not in favour of promoting him and did not approve of his ruthless approach towards people. Kadrin felt betrayed and tried to create mutiny but was crushed and cast out. His thirst for vengeance would serve Kharon well, as Kadrin had the skills and knowledge necessary to train an effective army.

Kharon paced his chamber, each step a reminder of the determination pulsing through his veins. The anticipation of the impending meeting at the Shadowed Vale filled him with energy, as he envisioned standing amongst those who would rally to his side.

Meanwhile, in Lucifer's kingdom, the atmosphere was a mixture of relief and uncertainty. Lucifer had fully healed from the battle against the Dark Lords, his strength renewed. He stood in the grand hall, surrounded by Leo, Valyron, and Kael, discussing the state of the kingdom.

"Now that the Dark Lords are vanquished, we can finally focus on rebuilding," Lucifer said, a hint of relief in his voice.

Kael nodded, looking at Lucifer with a mixture of admiration and concern. "But we must remain vigilant. There are whispers of unrest in the neighbouring kingdoms. Some may see our victory as a chance to reclaim what they lost."

Valyron crossed his arms, his brow furrowing. "It wouldn't surprise me if they conspired against us. We need to ensure that our defence are strong."

"Agreed," Leo added. "We must not let our guard down. If Kharon is still alive, we could be facing a threat we haven't fully comprehended."

Lucifer sighed, his thoughts drifting back to Kharon. "I had hoped he would find his way, but rejection can twist even the noblest of intentions. We must be prepared for anything."

As the four friends strategized, Kharon was busy executing his own plans, unaware that his actions would soon set in motion a chain of events that would bring both kingdoms to the brink of war.

Days passed, and Kharon received responses from some of the individuals he had reached out to. King Thessius was intrigued, though cautious. Queen Astrid expressed a fierce determination to join the cause, and Kadrin's reply was one of eager anticipation, ready to reclaim his lost honour.

The Call to Arms

With each confirmation, Kharon felt his confidence swell. He was assembling an army, a coalition of the wronged, and they would rise to challenge the ruler of Lightfall. The time for action was drawing near, and Kharon was ready to lead them into battle.

As the night of the meeting at the Shadowed Vale approached, Kharon stood before a mirror, adjusting his cloak. He looked at his reflection, seeing not just a man but a figure of vengeance and ambition. It was time to reclaim his place in the world and to prove to Lucifer that he was worthy—not just of acceptance, but of fear.

The meeting would mark the beginning of a new chapter, one where he would rise from the ashes of rejection and forge his destiny. The armies of the wronged would rally to him, and together, they would march against the golden spires of Lightfall, where a new dawn awaited.

24

SCHEMES OF THE SHADOWED SIEGE

*K*haron stood in the Shadowed Veil, a place concealed by darkness and seething with ancient power. The air here was thick with whispers from long-forgotten souls, and the leaders he summoned had finally arrived, each stepping into the dim chamber with hesitation and ambition. Kharon's eyes glimmered with a malevolent glow as he surveyed the figures before him: King Thessius, a ruthless monarch whose army had once ravaged kingdoms, Queen Astrid, a cunning and fearless leader of the most formidable navy in existence, and Kadrin, a silent but deadly sorcerer who had once pledged allegiance to Lucifer before betraying him.

"We are here to discuss the fall of Lucifer and his so-called kingdom," Kharon began, his voice low but commanding, filling the room like a looming storm. "Each of you has suffered because of him. Each of you has fought, only to see your efforts fail. But now, under my command, we will strike not only to win, but to break him completely." He allowed a pause, letting his words sink in.

From his cloak, Kharon unfurled a large, detailed map of Lucifer's castle and the surrounding lands. It was a map that none had seen before, drawn with precision that suggested he had spent countless hours studying every inch of Lucifer's kingdom, memorizing every vulnerability.

"We will hit him from all sides, leaving no escape, no mercy," Kharon said, his tone brimming with cruelty. He pointed to the map, tapping his fingers over the dense forests and mountainous terrain to the north. "King Thessius," he began, his gaze locking with the brutal king's eyes, "your army will march through these lands. The northern approach is guarded by thick forests, but once you push through, you'll find yourself on higher ground. That will be your advantage. Lucifer's ground forces are skilled, but they will crumble against the overwhelming numbers you possess. Burn the villages as you pass, destroy any outpost that stands in your way. Let fear spread through his people before you even reach the castle gates."

Thessius gave a wicked grin, the thought of terrorizing Lucifer's subjects already fuelling his cruel desires.

"And you, Queen Astrid," Kharon said, turning toward the naval commander. Her eyes narrowed, and she nodded slightly, awaiting her role. "Your fleet will sail down the eastern river that cuts through the lands. It's the quickest way to reach the castle from the sea. Lucifer has no navy, therefore that are being susceptible to danger. Once you break through, you'll launch a full-scale assault on the castle's eastern walls. The river itself will serve as a bloodline for your forces, feeding them into his castle like a flood. Surround his fortress with your ships, cut off any escape."

Astrid smirked, satisfied with her position in the scheme. She had long desired to take her naval might to the heart of Lucifer's kingdom, and now she would have the chance to obliterate him from the sea.

Kharon paused, letting the map's dark energy pulse beneath his fingertips. His expression darkened as he turned toward Kadrin, the sorcerer who had once called Lucifer a brother. "Kadrin, you and I will handle the most delicate part of this plan," Kharon said with a sinister edge. "We will attack his heart—the people closest to him. Valyron and Leo, his most trusted friends, will be our targets. They are the key to Lucifer's strength, the reason he holds on despite his kingdom crumbling around him." Kharon paused to find out the people in at his plan," If anyone is against this plan, may leave right now. But remember, this is your final chance to get your vengeance, to get what you deserved!"

Kadrin's lips twisted into a cruel smile. "I've long awaited this day," he said, agreeing to the plan and so did Astrid and Thessius.

"Valyron is a sorcerer of great skill," Kharon continued, "but he has one fatal flaw: his sense of loyalty. His bond with Lucifer blinds him to reason, and that is where we will strike. We will use magic not to attack him outright but to turn his own power against him. I will unleash an ancient curse upon Valyron, one that will eat away at his abilities, slowly but surely draining him of his strength. He will fight back, of course, but the more he uses his power, the faster the curse will consume him."

Kharon's gaze moved to Leo, a warrior known for his strength and strategy. "Leo, however, is different. He is a man of reason, a strategist. To defeat him, we will use deception. We will feed him false information, lure him into traps. He thrives on knowledge, and by corrupting the flow of information, we will make him question every move. With Leo paralyzed by doubt and Valyron weakened, Lucifer will be vulnerable."

The room was filled with a heavy silence as Kharon let his strategy unfold in their minds, each leader imagining the havoc they would unleash.

"And now," Kharon said, his voice growing darker, "to ensure Lucifer's downfall, we will make sure his kingdom is dismantled piece by piece. We will not attack in a single wave, but in a series of relentless strikes. Once King Thessius's forces overrun the northern approach, we will hold the high ground, forcing Lucifer's army to retreat. Queen Astrid, your fleet will rain fire upon the castle while it's under siege, and when the walls finally break, we will enter with overwhelming force."

He smiled wickedly, "But the real victory comes when we force Lucifer to watch as his kingdom falls apart. We will spread fear and chaos throughout the land, so that even his loyal subjects will question him. When his people start turning against him, that is when we will strike the final blow."

Kharon's words resonated with evil ambition, his eyes glinting with sadistic glee. He could already picture the fall of Lucifer, not just in body but in spirit.

"One last thing," Kharon said, looking around at the gathered leaders. "We attack at nighttime, giving them no time for preparation. We must be swift, for if we give Lucifer any time to recover, his strength will grow. The moment we leave this veil, you will begin your preparations. Thessius, your army should already be marching. Astrid, your ships should be ready to sail at dawn. Kadrin and I will strike at Valyron and Leo before the full assault begins. They will not see us coming."

With that, Kharon's dark plan was sealed, the fate of Lucifer hanging by a thread. Each leader departed with newfound resolve, ready to bring their forces to bear against the kingdom that had once stood strong. Kharon, now alone in the Veil, looked at the map one last time, a twisted smile on his lips.

"Lucifer," he whispered, "I will make you wish you had taken me in when you had the chance."

25

PRELUDE TO DESTRUCTION

$\mathcal{V}$alyron awoke in a cold sweat, his heart pounding in his chest. The vision was still vivid in his mind, a harrowing image of Kharon orchestrating the downfall of their kingdom, his destructive power threatening to annihilate everything they had fought to protect. The village burned, the people screaming in agony as flames licked at the once-peaceful homes. In his vision, Leo was caught in an iron grip, helpless and trapped. The sight of Lucifer, wounded and bleeding, haunted him the most. He couldn't shake the feeling of impending doom.

Breathing heavily, Valyron pushed the blankets aside and hurried to Lucifer's chamber. Time was of the essence; they had to act before it was too late. Bursting through the doors, he found Lucifer seated at the end of a long table, maps of the kingdom and its surrounding regions sprawled before him. His eyes, though sharp, still held traces of exhaustion from the last battle.

"Lucifer," Valyron said, his voice shaking. "We're in grave danger."

Lucifer looked up, sensing the urgency in his tone. "What's happened?"

"I've had a vision. Kharon is coming for us, and he's bringing destruction like we've never seen before. Our village… the people… they'll burn. Leo will be captured, and we will all be killed if we don't act now!"

Lucifer stood, concern deepening the lines on his face. "Tell me everything."

Valyron quickly recounted the images from his vision—the sight of Kharon standing at the helm of an army, sending out orders to leaders of distant kingdoms. The attack would be from all sides. King Thessius would strike by land, Queen Astrid's navy would assault their shores, and Kharon himself, alongside Kadrin, would come for their dearest allies, Leo and Valyron.

"We have no time to waste," Valyron said, pacing the room. "I saw it clearly. We must strengthen our defence. We need a powerful navy to defend our shores, or we'll be overwhelmed."

Lucifer rubbed his chin, his mind already formulating a plan. "If Kharon is uniting our enemies, it means he's looking to strike where we are weakest."

"And that's why we need Kael," Valyron said, locking eyes with Lucifer. "We need his strength, his resources. We must send a message for him to bring as much backup as he can, including a navy. And we must evacuate the villagers—send them to Kael's village, far away from the front lines. If they stay, they'll die."

Lucifer nodded. "You're right. Kharon's assault will be devastating if we're not prepared. We'll send word to Kael immediately." He paused, his expression darkening. "But this war… it's going to take everything we have. Kharon isn't just after land. He's after blood."

Valyron clenched his fists. "He's angry, driven by vengeance. I felt it in the vision. This attack is personal for him, especially against us. Leo and I are his prime targets."

Lucifer crossed the room to the open window, gazing out at the village below. The peaceful sight of villagers going about their daily tasks, unaware of the storm about to descend upon them, weighed heavy on his heart. He couldn't allow their lives to be lost in this senseless war. They had already sacrificed too much.

"We'll send a call to Kael," Lucifer said decisively. "He'll answer. We need his armies, his ships, and his wisdom. The villagers will be evacuated to his lands, where they'll be safe. As for here, we'll fortify our defence, train every able-bodied person, and prepare for the worst. If Kharon wants to wage war, we'll give him a fight he'll never forget."

Valyron nodded, feeling the tension in the air tighten. "I'll start the preparations. Leo should be warned as well. We can't afford to lose any more time."

Lucifer placed a hand on Valyron's shoulder, sensing the weight of the responsibility his friend bore. "We'll get through this. Kharon might be powerful, but he's not unbeatable. We've faced worse, and we've come out victorious. This will be no different."

Valyron tried to find comfort in Lucifer's words, but the dark images of his vision still lingered in his mind. He knew this battle would be unlike any they had fought before. It wasn't just about power or strategy; it was about Kharon's deeply personal grudge, a desire for vengeance that had twisted him beyond recognition.

The following hours were a whirlwind of preparation. A messenger was sent to Kael, carrying Lucifer's request for reinforcements and a naval fleet. Valyron personally saw to the evacuation of the villagers, ensuring they were safely on their way to Kael's lands. Women, children, and the elderly were hurried onto carts and ships, their frightened faces a reminder of what was at stake. Every able-bodied man and woman who could fight was armed and brought into makeshift training camps to prepare for the inevitable battle.

Leo, upon hearing Valyron's vision, was grim but resolute. "Kharon might think he can defeat us, but he's underestimating our strength. We've faced worse enemies than him."

"We need to be ready for anything," Valyron said. "This isn't just about brute strength. Kharon is calculating, and he knows our weaknesses."

Leo narrowed his eyes. "Then we won't give him the chance to exploit them."

As the last of the villagers were evacuated, Lucifer and his commanders gathered in the war room, a large chamber lined with maps, weapons, and strategic documents. Kael's response had been swift—his armies and ships were already on the way. But they needed a strategy that would not only defend their lands but also counter Kharon's multi-pronged attack.

"We'll divide our forces," Valyron said, standing over the map. "Leo and I will take the frontline to deal with Thessius's army. Our navy, bolstered by Kael's ships, will handle Astrid's forces on the water. Lucifer, you'll stay at the heart of the kingdom, overseeing all fronts. Kharon will come for you, but we'll make sure he never gets close."

Lucifer nodded, his expression grim but determined. "We fight with everything we have. There's no room for error."

The air was heavy with anticipation, every breath carrying the weight of the coming conflict. As they finalized their plans, Valyron's thoughts kept drifting back to his vision—Leo's capture, the burning village, Lucifer's fall. They had done everything they could to prepare, but would it be enough?

As the night fell and the fires of the kingdom's forges blazed into the dark sky, Valyron stood at the window, staring out at the distant horizon. Somewhere out there, Kharon was preparing his assault, gathering his allies, and readying himself for war. Valyron could feel the storm approaching, and he only hoped they could withstand its fury.

26

THE STRATEGIST'S GAMBIT

*V*alyron's workspace was a flurry of movement. Herbs, enchanted stones, and vials of various liquids bubbled and hissed over his table as he meticulously crafted potions for the upcoming battle. The air was thick with the smell of magic, sharp and pungent, as he mixed and stirred, his brow furrowed in concentration.

"This will do," he muttered to himself, carefully measuring out the last ingredient—essence of wyvern fang, a rare and dangerous component that amplified the strength of any mixture it touched. The concoction in front of him glowed faintly in the dim light, a sickly green, pulsing with life. It was a potion designed to flow through the veins like fire, burning out any poison, sickness, or weakness that might plague the body. More than that, it enhanced strength and aggression, perfect for battle. It made a soldier into a war machine.

Valyron wiped the sweat from his brow, taking a deep breath before setting the finished vials aside. "Lucifer will need this more than anyone," he whispered, thinking of their leader's recent trials. The war against the Dark Lords had taken its toll, but Lucifer had pushed through, leading them with unyielding resolve. Still, Valyron knew the battle ahead would be even more dangerous, especially with Kharon now seeking revenge.

Just as he was preparing the next set of potions for Kael and the rest of the army, Leo burst into the room, his face alight with urgency. "Valyron!" he called, his voice echoing in the chamber. "I've thought of a new plan."

Valyron looked up, his hands still covered in potion residue, raising an eyebrow. "Another revision?" he asked, though his tone carried no mockery. Leo was always the strategist, constantly refining and perfecting their battle approach.

"Yes, this might give us the upper hand," Leo said, pacing as he spoke. "I remembered one of the great Roman wars. The Romans were outnumbered, but they struck their enemy's heart—the throne. It forced the enemy to retreat and defend, which led to their downfall. We can use a similar strategy against Kharon. I have already let Lucifer know about this plan"

Valyron's eyes narrowed with interest as he agreed, Leo continued, "We send Kael with one-fourth of the army to Kharon's throne, to attack his base of power. While he's distracted defending it, the navy will be handled by me. You will take charge of the rest of the army and stand by for the land battle. But there's more," Leo paused, glancing at Valyron to gauge his reaction.

Valyron crossed his arms, nodding for Leo to go on.

"I need you to be especially careful," Leo continued, his voice lowering. "There's a chance we may need Draco, our loyal dragon, to lead the final charge. If it comes to that, we'll have to use everything we have." Leo's tone was filled with an unspoken understanding—they were preparing for the worst.

Valyron smirked. "Draco will thrash any enemy that stands before him. You know that," he said confidently. "But if you think this revised plan will work, we'll need to act quickly. Kharon is dangerous, but if we take out his throne while he's distracted, we have a real shot."

Leo nodded, glancing at the shimmering potions on Valyron's table. "And those will help," he added, pointing to the vials. "What's in them?"

"A cure for any poison," Valyron replied, picking up one of the bottles and swirling it in front of Leo. "It purges any venom from the bloodstream, but it also gives the user a temporary boost—strength, endurance, and a touch of aggression. It'll turn our soldiers into something more… dangerous."

Leo took a vial from Valyron's hand, inspecting it closely. "We'll need every edge we can get."

Valyron turned back to his work, quickly finishing the last of the potions. "Three per soldier. That should be enough to get them through the battle," he said, neatly lining up the completed vials in rows.

Just then, Kael entered the room, his eyes scanning the preparations. "So, there you are," Leo greeted him with a nod. "We've made a slight change to the plan."

Kael folded his arms across his chest. "Oh?"

Leo gestured for him to come closer, explaining the revised strategy. "You'll lead one-fourth of the army to Kharon's throne. Attack it directly—force him to defend it. While you keep him distracted, I'll take command of the navy, and Valyron will hold the line with the rest of our forces."

Kael's expression grew serious as he absorbed the information. "Attacking the throne... risky, but effective if we time it right," he said thoughtfully. "And what of the dragon? Do you think Draco will respond when the time comes?"

"Draco is more than ready," Valyron interjected. "When we call for him, he'll strike like a storm."

Kael gave a curt nod. "Then it's settled. We move at dawn."

The air was thick with the weight of their decision. Leo, Valyron, and Kael stood together in the dimly lit chamber, surrounded by the tools of war—potions, weapons, and strategy. They had a plan, but they all knew that once the battle began, anything could happen.

Valyron handed Kael a set of potions. "Take these," he said. "Three per person. It'll keep your soldiers alive and fighting longer."

Kael accepted the vials, tucking them away carefully. "Let's hope we don't need too many of them."

Leo clapped a hand on Kael's shoulder. "We've got this. Kharon won't know what hit him."

But beneath his confident exterior, Leo knew the gravity of what lay ahead. He glanced at Valyron, seeing the same thoughts reflected in his friend's eyes.

This was more than just a battle—it was a turning point. Their fates would be decided in the coming hours.

As they finalized their preparations, the quiet hum of war readiness settled over them. The kingdom, still recovering from the last battle, braced itself for the storm that was about to hit.

Leo looked out of the window toward the horizon, where the faintest glimmer of dawn was just beginning to touch the sky. "Whatever happens," he said softly, "we fight for our future."

27

THE BATTLE UNFOLDS

The sky was dim, casting a pale light over the battlefield as the day of reckoning had come. The village, once alive with the sound of chatter and the buzz of everyday life, now stood in eerie silence. Smoke billowed in the distance, and the smell of burnt wood and ash filled the air as King Thessius led his forces towards the village. Flames rose high, licking the sky as he ordered his soldiers to set fire to everything in their path, reducing homes and barns to rubble. His dark eyes scanned the burning horizon, but something felt off—there were no cries, no signs of life.

The villagers were gone.

The realization hit him like a stone to the chest. His plan to terrify and weaken Lucifer's kingdom by attacking its most vulnerable—the common people—had failed. Thessius clenched his fists, his eyes narrowing as he spat out orders. "It's a trick," he growled, his voice dripping with frustration. "They've evacuated. We've been outplayed."

Meanwhile, far off the coast, Queen Astrid stood aboard the deck of her flagship. The naval force was an awe-inspiring sight—a fleet of mighty warships, each bristling with cannons and battle-hardened soldiers. The queen, regal and composed, watched the horizon with a cold, calculating gaze. She was certain that Lucifer's forces wouldn't expect an assault from the sea. They were prepared for a land invasion, not a naval strike.

But then, the shape of a navy emerged from the mist. Astrid's eyes widened in surprise. "So, they were ready for us after all," she muttered, a grin curling her lips. "But it won't be enough."

The Battle Unfolds

Her ships charged forward, cannons roaring to life as the battle on the sea began. The clash of steel, the thunder of cannon fire, and the cries of soldiers filled the air. Astrid's forces were formidable, and despite the preparation of Lucifer's navy, they struggled to match the ferocity of her attack. One by one, their ships fell, swallowed by the sea. But even as they sank, Leo's navy fought valiantly, refusing to go down without a fight.

On land, Valyron watched the flames consume the empty village. He had expected as much. The villagers had been safely evacuated, just as he and Leo had planned. But now, the real challenge was upon them. King Thessius' army was approaching fast, and Valyron knew that this was where the true test of their strength would come.

With a sharp intake of breath, he felt the familiar rush of the potion coursing through his veins. The concoction he had carefully crafted, designed to heighten their senses, increase their strength, and dull the pain of their wounds, had worked as intended. He could feel its effects—the sharpness of his mind, the quickening of his reflexes, the way the pain from his earlier injuries seemed to fade into the background.

But as he surveyed the approaching army, Valyron knew that even with the potion's power, they were vastly outnumbered. He wasn't scared, though. Not anymore. He had faced death many times before, and if today was the day he fell, then he would fall fighting.

His hand tightened around his staff, and he looked at Leo, who stood beside him, his eyes sharp and focused. "Are you ready?" Valyron asked.

Leo nodded, his jaw set. "Always."

Valyron let out a long breath. "Then let's make this count."

The two men, standing side by side, felt the tension in the air grow thick. The sounds of war echoed in the distance, but here, in the heart of the kingdom, it was only a matter of time before the battle reached them. Valyron's mind raced, thinking of every possible outcome, every contingency. But in the end, there was no time for second-guessing.

"Hold the line," Leo commanded, his voice ringing out across the battlefield as their army prepared for the clash. "We won't let them take a single step further."

As the soldiers lined up, gripping their swords and shields tightly, Valyron could see the determination in their eyes. These were not mere men—they were warriors, each one willing to lay down their life for the kingdom. Valyron's heart swelled with pride.

And then, the enemy arrived.

Thessius' forces charged, the ground shaking beneath their feet. The two armies collided with a deafening crash, and chaos erupted. Steel met steel, and the air was filled with the clang of weapons, the cries of the wounded, and the thundering beat of hooves.

Valyron fought like a man possessed. His staff moved in a blur, deflecting blows and sending enemies flying with bursts of magic. He was injured—his arm was bleeding from a deep gash, and his leg ached from an earlier strike—but he didn't let it slow him down. In fact, the pain only fuelled his fury. He fought like a wounded lion—dangerous and relentless.

Leo, too, was in the thick of the battle. His sword was a blur of motion, cutting through enemies with deadly precision. He had taken hits—his armour was dented, and blood stained his side—but the potion kept him going. He could feel the strength surging through him, keeping him on his feet, driving him forward.

And yet, even with all their power, they were being pushed back.

"They're too strong," Valyron shouted over the din of battle, his voice strained. "We need more time!"

Leo gritted his teeth, cutting down another enemy before turning to Valyron. "Then we'll give them hell until Kael arrives!"

But Kael was still far off, leading a portion of the army to Kharon's throne as per the plan. Leo's mind raced. The strategy had been sound—dividing their forces to hit Kharon's stronghold while defending the kingdom. But now,

The Battle Unfolds

standing in the thick of battle, he wondered if they had underestimated the enemy's strength.

Suddenly, a horn sounded from the distance. Queen Astrid's navy had arrived, her ships now docking at the kingdom's shores. Leo's heart sank as he watched her forces pour onto the land. Their defence was crumbling, and now they were being attacked from both land and sea.

Valyron, bloodied and battered, stood beside him, breathing heavily. "We can't hold them off much longer," he said, wiping sweat from his brow. His body was screaming in pain, but he refused to give in.

Just then, Draco, the mighty dragon, soared overhead, letting out a deafening roar. The sight of the creature bolstered their spirits. Leo looked up at the dragon with a mixture of awe and relief. "Draco," he whispered. "Now's the time."

The dragon swooped low, unleashing torrents of fire upon the enemy forces, scattering them in all directions. Soldiers screamed as they were engulfed in flames, and the enemy's advance was momentarily halted.

Leo seized the opportunity. "Valyron!" he shouted. "Now's our chance!"

With renewed vigour, the two men charged forward, cutting down anyone who stood in their way. They fought like demons, refusing to let the kingdom fall.

But even as they pushed back the enemy, Leo knew that this was just the beginning. The real threat was still out there—Kharon, lurking in the shadows, waiting for his moment to strike.

As the sun began to set, casting an eerie red glow over the battlefield, Leo and Valyron stood together, breathing heavily. The battle was far from over, and they both knew it. But they were ready. They had to be.

Because if they failed, the kingdom would fall, and all would be lost.

And somewhere, hidden in the distance, Kharon watched, a sinister smile creeping across his face as his plan unfolded exactly as he had envisioned.

28

THE BATTLE UNFOLDS: PART II

The evening air thickened with tension as the sun's last rays bled across the sky, casting an ominous glow on the battlefield. Kharon, cloaked in shadows atop a distant hill, observed the chaos below with a cold, calculating gaze. Everything was unfolding as planned. His enemies were stretched thin, their defence faltering. He could almost taste victory.

The armies of Thessius and Astrid had delivered a significant blow, and yet, Lucifer's forces were fighting with a resilience that vexed him. They should have crumbled by now. Kharon's dark eyes flickered with impatience as he watched Draco unleash hellfire from above, scattering his troops.

"This isn't how it ends," Kharon whispered, a sneer curling on his lips. "Not today."

He raised a hand, and from the shadows emerged Kadrin, the cloaked figure who had been silently awaiting his command. Kadrin's piercing eyes gleamed under the hood, his sinister smile mirroring Kharon's own malice.

"We've weakened them enough," Kharon said, his voice low and menacing. "Now, it's time to strike where it truly hurts."

Kadrin nodded, his presence a chilling reminder of the evil that had awakened. Together, they descended from their vantage point, slipping through the shadows like ghosts, unseen and unstoppable. Their target was clear—Valyron and Leo. Kharon had studied his enemies well; he knew that Lucifer's closest allies were the heart of his strength. Remove them, and the rest would crumble.

The Battle Unfolds: Part II

Meanwhile, back at the battlefield, Leo and Valyron continued to fight with all their might, their bodies aching, their minds clouded with exhaustion, but the potion still surged through their veins, giving them just enough to keep pushing forward. Draco circled overhead, swooping down periodically to drive back the enemy, but even the mighty dragon could not stop the relentless tide.

Valyron wiped blood from his brow, glancing around at the battered soldiers. "This can't go on much longer," he muttered to Leo. "We're barely holding them off."

Leo nodded grimly, his jaw tight. "We have no choice. We hold the line until Kael returns with reinforcements."

The sound of crashing waves and roaring fires echoed in the distance as Queen Astrid's forces continued their naval assault, systematically taking down the remaining defence along the coast. In the thick of the action, Astrid herself stood at the prow of her flagship, her eyes scanning the battlefield with cold satisfaction.

"Send word to Kharon," she commanded her second-in-command. "Tell him the castle will soon be vulnerable. We await his final command."

Her messenger hurried off, disappearing into the chaos.

As the battle raged on, Valyron's senses suddenly sharpened, his vision flickering as an unsettling chill crept up his spine. The air seemed to grow colder, darker. His heart pounded in his chest, and for a brief moment, time seemed to slow.

A vision struck him like lightning.

He saw Kharon, standing amidst the ruins of the kingdom, his cruel laughter echoing as flames consumed the land. Valyron saw himself and Leo, lying motionless amidst the destruction, the kingdom they swore to protect reduced to ashes. And Draco—Draco was nowhere to be seen.

Valyron gasped, snapping back to reality, his eyes wide with terror. "Leo," he breathed, grabbing his friend's arm. "We need to go—now. Kharon is coming. He's going to kill us, burn the village, trap you"

Leo's eyes narrowed, the urgency in Valyron's voice snapping him to attention. He interrupted ignoring the last few words Valyron said about him, "Then we need to be prepared."

"We don't have enough soldiers!" Valyron spat, panic rising in his voice. "We need Kael, we need backup, we need—"

"Calm down," Leo said firmly, gripping Valyron's shoulder. "We'll send the call to Kael for reinforcements. You said it yourself—he'll come."

Valyron's breath came fast, but he nodded. He knew that Leo was right. Panic wouldn't help them now. They needed to think clearly, act quickly, or they'd lose everything.

Leo wasted no time, dispatching a trusted scout with a message to Kael, urging him to bring every soldier and ship he could muster. "And bring Draco," Leo added, his eyes flashing with determination. "We'll need him if this goes south."

As the scout vanished into the fray, Valyron moved with renewed purpose. "I'm going to make more of those potions," he said, his voice tight with resolve. "We'll need every advantage we can get. Meet me in the war room when the scout returns."

Leo nodded, his mind already working on the next step. He could feel the weight of the upcoming battle pressing down on him. The war hadn't even truly begun yet, and they were already struggling. But if there was one thing Leo knew for sure, it was that they wouldn't go down without a fight.

Hours passed, and as night fell over the war-torn kingdom, Kharon made his move. His forces were gathered at the Shadowed Veil, a place shrouded in mystery and dark magic. The leaders of the kingdoms that had opposed Lucifer—King Thessius, Queen Astrid, and the warlord Kadrin—stood before him, awaiting his final orders.

Kharon unfurled the map he had meticulously drawn, a detailed schematic of Lucifer's kingdom and the surrounding areas. His voice was low, dripping with venom as he explained his plan one final time.

The Battle Unfolds: Part II

"We will strike from all sides," Kharon began, his finger tracing the outline of the castle on the map. "King Thessius, you will lead the land assault, burning everything in your path. Leave no building standing. Queen Astrid, your navy will launch a full-scale attack on their coastal defence, ensuring that no reinforcements can reach them by sea. Kadrin and I…" Kharon's smile widened, a gleam of malice in his eyes. "We will go after Valyron and Leo. Without them, Lucifer is nothing."

Kharon paused, letting his words sink in. The leaders exchanged glances, each one aware of the magnitude of the plan. But there was no turning back now.

"We hit hard, we hit fast," Kharon continued, his tone commanding. "Lucifer will fall, and with him, the kingdom. This land will be ours to rule."

King Thessius nodded, his eyes gleaming with bloodlust. "Consider it done."

Queen Astrid smirked, her confidence unwavering. "Their navy is no match for mine."

Kadrin, standing silently beside Kharon, merely smiled—an expression devoid of warmth, a promise of death.

Kharon rolled up the map, his eyes scanning the faces of his allies. "Prepare your armies. Tomorrow, we will unleash hell."

As the leaders left the Shadowed Veil, Kharon remained, staring out into the night. His mind raced, thoughts of revenge swirling in his head. Lucifer had made a grave mistake in rejecting him, and now he would pay the ultimate price.

Tomorrow, the kingdom would fall. And Kharon would be the one to bring it to its knees.

29

THE MADNESS OF WAR

The kingdom was eerily quiet, the stillness only broken by the occasional clank of armour and hurried whispers of soldiers preparing for war. The air was thick with tension, as though the very land itself held its breath, waiting for the coming destruction.

Inside the castle, Valyron moved swiftly, his fingers deftly measuring ingredients, crushing leaves, and stirring potions. Each vial he prepared shimmered faintly in the dim light of the chamber, the liquid within glowing with a faint green hue. These were no ordinary potions; they were his finest work, designed to turn the tide of battle. He had mixed them with elements of rare herbs, arcane components, and a touch of his own magic.

"They will need these," he muttered to himself, bottling the last vial and placing it on the shelf with the others. He glanced out the window, his brow furrowed with worry. The vision still haunted him—the fire, the destruction, the overwhelming sense of helplessness. He couldn't let it come to pass.

There was a knock on the door, and Leo entered, his face grim but determined. "Valyron, how are the potions coming?"

"They're ready," Valyron said, his voice steady despite the growing anxiety gnawing at him. "Each soldier will have three vials. It'll enhance their strength, endurance, and even heal minor wounds. But be warned—the effects come at a cost. The longer they fight under the potion's influence, the more aggressive and reckless they may become."

Leo nodded, understanding the risk. "We'll need every advantage we can get."

Valyron handed him a pouch filled with vials. "For you. Drink it when you feel like you're running out of energy. But don't overuse it, Leo. It could drive you to madness if you're not careful."

Leo took the pouch, his expression hardening. "We can't afford to hold back now. Kharon is coming with everything he's got."

Valyron looked up at him, his eyes filled with concern. "Have we heard from Kael?"

Leo shook his head. "Not yet, but he'll come. He has to."

A heavy silence fell between them. Both knew what was at stake, and both understood the weight of the decisions they had made. They had sent the villagers away, hoping to protect them from the carnage that was about to unfold. But the kingdom itself—they would have to defend it to the last man.

Leo moved to the window, his gaze fixed on the horizon. The sky was dark, storm clouds gathering in the distance. It was as if the heavens themselves were preparing for the battle.

"We'll hold them off, Valyron," Leo said quietly. "We've fought worse odds before."

Valyron joined him at the window, his eyes scanning the empty streets below. "I've seen what's coming, Leo. This isn't like anything we've faced. Kharon… he's different. He's not just powerful—he's angry. And he's smart. He won't fight fair."

Leo's jaw clenched. "Then we'll be smarter."

There was another knock at the door, and a scout entered, panting from his run. "Sir, we've spotted Queen Astrid's navy approaching from the west. They'll be here by dawn."

Leo's face darkened. "How many ships?"

"Dozens, sir. Her entire fleet."

Leo nodded. "Get the archers and sorcerers ready. We'll meet them head-on."

The scout saluted and hurried off, leaving Leo and Valyron in the thick silence of the war room.

Valyron turned to Leo, his face set with grim determination. "What's the plan?"

Leo exhaled slowly, his mind working through the strategy they had devised. "Kael should be here by morning. We'll split the forces. You and I will defend the castle, hold off Kharon's ground forces. Kael will take a detachment to Kharon's stronghold—strike at the heart of his power."

"And the navy?"

"I'll handle it. Queen Astrid is strong, but I know her tactics. We'll give her a fight she won't expect."

Valyron nodded, his heart heavy but resolute. "And Kharon?"

Leo's eyes darkened. "Kharon is mine."

The hours crawled by, the castle a flurry of activity as preparations were made. Soldiers donned their armour, sharpening their weapons and exchanging quiet words of encouragement. The tension was palpable, the anticipation of the coming battle weighing heavily on everyone.

As dawn approached, Valyron stood atop the castle walls, watching the first light of morning break over the horizon. In the distance, he could see the faint outlines of ships approaching—Queen Astrid's navy, cutting through the waters like a swarm of sharks. Beyond that, he could see the dust clouds rising from the ground—Kharon's forces, marching toward the castle with relentless precision.

Valyron's heart raced, his fingers tightening around the staff in his hand. He had prepared for this. He had trained for this. But nothing could truly prepare him for the sight of the army that awaited them.

Beside him, Leo stood tall, his face grim but resolute. "It's time."

Valyron nodded, his voice steady despite the fear gnawing at his insides. "We're ready."

The first horn sounded, signalling the start of the attack. The regiment led by Leo, launched from the high land, their spells arrows and explosions cutting through the waves to meet Queen Astrid's forces head-on. Valyron watched as the two fleets clashed in a violent storm of fire and steel, the sound of cannons and the roar of battle filling the air.

On land, Kharon's army surged forward, crashing against the castle's defence like a tidal wave. Valyron's heart pounded in his chest as he raised his staff, summoning a shield of energy to protect the walls. He could feel the strain of the magic, but he pushed through it, knowing that they couldn't afford to let the enemy break through.

Leo fought beside him, his sword a blur of motion as he cut down wave after wave of attackers. The potion coursed through his veins, giving him the strength to fight on, even as his body screamed in protest.

But Kharon was nowhere to be seen.

Valyron's eyes scanned the battlefield, searching for any sign of the dark sorcerer. He knew Kharon wouldn't attack directly. He was waiting, watching, planning.

And then, out of the corner of his eye, Valyron saw him—a shadow moving through the ranks of soldiers, slipping past the chaos unnoticed.

"Kharon," Valyron whispered, his eyes narrowing.

Leo followed his gaze, his face darkening. "He's here."

Without another word, they both moved, slipping through the battlefield toward the figure cloaked in shadows. This was the moment they had been waiting for—the final confrontation with the man who had threatened to destroy everything they had fought for.

As they approached, Kharon turned, his eyes gleaming with malice.

"You're too late," he said, his voice cold and mocking. "The kingdom will fall."

Valyron raised his staff, his magic crackling in the air. "Not while we still stand." Kharon smiled, a cruel, twisted smile. "Then you'll die standing." And with that, the battle for the kingdom truly began.

30

WRATH OF THE FALLEN

The battlefield was chaos. Kharon, in the centre of the storm, wielded his dark powers, tearing through Lucifer's forces. His eyes gleamed with unbridled rage, each blow delivered with deadly precision. Soldiers crumbled before him, their defence shattered, as he unleashed the full force of his anger.

Amidst the clashing swords and screams of the fallen, the sound of hooves pounded the earth. A war horse, black as the night, charged forward through the smoke, carrying Kael. His eyes locked onto Kharon, and with a booming voice, he shouted above the roar of battle, "Kharon! Stop at once!"

Kharon paused mid-strike, turning to face Kael. His face twisted in disdain. "You dare interrupt me, Kael? You're too late. Your army crumbles beneath my might. Soon, Lucifer and his allies will fall."

Kael, undeterred, raised his hand, signalling his troops to stand firm. He steered his horse closer to Kharon, who stood tall amidst the bodies of fallen soldiers.

"You think this war is yours to win?" Kael's voice was sharp and cold. "A war is not won through power alone, Kharon. It is won through intelligence and strategy."

Kharon narrowed his eyes. "You think I care for your games, Kael? My power is enough to crush you all."

Kael laughed, a harsh, mocking sound that echoed across the battlefield. "You may have burned our villages, but not our people. You may have attacked our castle, but your navy couldn't destroy it. Your plan, Kharon... it has already failed."

For the first time, uncertainty flickered in Kharon's eyes.

Kael continued, riding circles around him. "While you were obsessed with unleashing your fury on our forces, we've been two steps ahead. I bring news you did not expect." He leaned in closer, his voice dropping into a dangerous whisper, loud enough only for Kharon to hear. "No person in your kingdom remains alive. Your throne has been reduced to ash."

Kharon's eyes widened with disbelief, his hands trembling slightly on the hilt of his weapon. "What are you saying?" he hissed, trying to maintain his composure.

Kael's smile was cold and unrelenting. "Your kingdom, your people, your precious throne—it's all gone. We burned everything. Every last thing you once cherished has been reduced to rubble."

For a moment, Kharon stood still, his breath shallow as the realization sank in. His entire kingdom, wiped out while he had been consumed by his hatred for Lucifer. His mind raced, a flood of memories and emotions crashing over him. The whole time he built power, planned his revenge, had now crumbled in mere moments.

Kharon's hands clenched around his sword, his knuckles white with fury. "You... you lie!"

Kael shook his head, unfazed. "Send your men back, Kharon, if you wish. But you'll find nothing but ash."

Kharon's face twisted in rage, his eyes burning with hatred as he pointed his sword toward Kael. "You think you've won something, Kael? I'll bury you in this very ground."

"You've already lost, Kharon," Kael retorted. "This war isn't about who's stronger anymore—it's about who's left standing. And you're standing alone."

Kharon let out a roar of fury and swung his sword at Kael, who expertly parried the strike. Sparks flew as their blades collided, the tension between them thickening. Kharon's eyes were wild, the weight of his failure driving him into a frenzy.

Suddenly, Valyron appeared, emerging from the chaos, his staff glowing with arcane energy. "Kharon, enough!" he shouted. "Look around you—your forces are crumbling! You've lost everything. It's over."

But Kharon wasn't listening. His gaze was fixed solely on Kael, consumed by the desire to kill the man who had taken everything from him. He charged at Kael again, faster this time, his strikes wild but filled with power.

Kael gritted his teeth, blocking each blow with effort. "You're fighting a battle you've already lost!" he spat, his breath laboured as he struggled to keep up with Kharon's unrelenting assault.

Leo's voice rang out from the distance. "Kael, get back!"

In a flash, Draco soared overhead, letting out a bone-rattling roar that shook the ground beneath them. The earth trembled as the massive dragon swooped low, sending gusts of wind across the battlefield. Kharon faltered, momentarily distracted by the sheer force of the dragon's presence.

That was the opening they needed. Lucifer, who had been watching from afar, charged forward with inhuman speed. His sword gleamed in the dim light as he dashed towards Kharon. With a powerful, swift stroke, Lucifer's blade struck Kharon's back, forcing the dark sorcerer to stumble forward.

Valyron quickly followed, hurling bolts of arcane energy to disorient Kharon further, while Leo circled around to flank him. Together, they closed in on him, surrounding him from all sides. Kharon, cornered and wounded, snarled in defiance. "You think you can defeat me? You're fools!" Kharon let out an evil laugh and said, "What you people never understand and never will is, there is always a plan B. I have something for you all. They will strike once you are weak. Once you are vulnerable." Lucifer stepped forward, his expression cold and unyielding. "This ends now, Kharon. You have nothing left. "With a final roar, Draco unleashed a deafening bellow that reverberated through the battlefield, shaking the ground like an earthquake. Kharon, thrown off balance by the dragon's fury, staggered, his grip on his weapon weakening.

Lucifer's eyes blazed with fury as he raised his sword high. "For my people. For my kingdom."

He brought his sword down with a mighty swing, cutting through Kharon's defence with ease. The blade slashed across Kharon's chest, and blood sprayed into the air. Kharon gasped, his body trembling as he struggled to remain standing. Lucifer didn't stop. He swung his sword again and again, each strike faster and more precise than the last. His movements were a blur as he ensured that Kharon would never rise again. By the time Lucifer stopped, Kharon lay in pieces, scattered across the blood-soaked battlefield. The dark sorcerer, who had once threatened to destroy everything Lucifer held dear, was no more.

For a moment, the battlefield was silent. Then, as if signalling the end of the battle, Draco let out one final roar, a victorious cry that echoed into the distance. Lucifer, bloodied and breathing heavily, wiped the blood from his face and turned to his allies. "It's over," he said quietly, his voice filled with exhaustion and relief. Kael, Leo, and Valyron stood beside him, weary but victorious. They had fought through hell and emerged on the other side. The Dark Lords were finished, and Kharon's reign of terror had come to an end.

But the scars of the war would remain forever etched in their minds.

31

THE END OF AN ERA: THE NEW PROCLAMATION

The war had left them all shattered, not just physically but emotionally. For days, the remnants of the battlefield still echoed in their minds—the sounds of steel clashing, men screaming, and the sight of their comrades falling one by one. The guilt weighed heavily on their hearts.

Lucifer, once proud and invincible, stood at the edge of the war-torn landscape, staring blankly at the horizon. His once radiant, confident face was now shadowed with exhaustion. The man who had led them through countless battles, the man they all believed could never falter, now seemed broken. His hands trembled slightly, and his eyes were filled with the ghosts of the war they had just survived.

Valyron, Leo, and Kael were by his side, equally consumed by their own thoughts. They had fought valiantly. They had won. But at what cost?

Leo was the first to speak, his voice quiet yet burdened with the weight of his guilt. "We could have saved more… there were moments when… I—" He trailed off, unable to finish his sentence. The faces of fallen soldiers flashed in his mind. Those he had trained, men he had shared laughter with. And now they were gone.

Valyron, gripping his staff, said nothing but his expression spoke volumes. His usual sharp wit and energy had dulled in the aftermath of the battle. He'd brewed potions to strengthen them, to heal them, but he could not heal what war had done to their souls.

Kael, usually the most stoic of the group, sighed heavily. "No matter how many victories, it feels like every war brings us closer to defeat. We saved many lives, but... how many did we lose?"

The silence after Kael's words was suffocating, filled with unsaid regrets and unspoken pain. The four of them stood there, lost in their own spiralling thoughts, before Lucifer finally broke the silence.

"I'm done," he said, his voice cracking slightly as if admitting the truth to himself hurt more than any blade could. "I can't do this anymore."

Leo, Valyron, and Kael turned toward him, disbelief in their eyes.

Lucifer continued, his tone heavy with finality. "No war is justified. Not this one, not the last, not the next. We've fought for too long, killed for too long. And I've led you all into battles that should never have been fought. I... I need to stop." He shook his head slowly. "I have to retire."

The words hung in the air, cold and unforgiving.

Valyron's face showed a flicker of surprise, then concern. "Lucifer, you're the strongest among us. If you leave, who will lead?"

Lucifer turned to face them, his eyes tired but resolute. "Someone else. Someone who hasn't been worn down by this endless cycle of violence. I've given enough, we've all given enough." He paused, his voice dropping as if speaking to himself more than them. "I've given too much."

Kael frowned. "But what will happen to the kingdom? To the people who still need you?"

Lucifer gazed out into the distance, his expression far away. "I've been a ruler, a fighter, for so long that I've forgotten what it's like to just... live. To have peace, real peace. This war... it was different. I don't feel victorious. I feel guilty." His hands clenched into fists. "This wasn't just a battle, it was a massacre. And we've become numb to it. How many more lives have to be destroyed for us to realize no victory is worth this?"

Leo stepped forward, his voice shaking slightly. "You can't blame yourself for this war, Lucifer. We all agreed it had to be fought."

"And I led you into it. I was the one who said we had no other choice. But maybe there was another way, maybe we could have stopped this before it began."

The silence returned, and for a long moment, no one knew what to say. The weight of Lucifer's words was almost too much to bear.

Valyron finally spoke, his voice quiet but firm. "If you retire..., what will you do?"

Lucifer chuckled, though there was no humour in it. "I don't know. Maybe find a place far from here. A place where I can think, breathe... live a life without this burden."

Kael crossed his arms, his brow furrowed. "And what about us? What about the kingdom? You can't just leave everything behind."

Lucifer looked at them, his old friends, his comrades, the people who had stood by his side through every trial. His heart ached with the thought of abandoning them. "You're stronger than you think, Kael. You all are. You don't need me anymore. The kingdom doesn't need a king who's lost faith in war."

Leo looked torn. "But we've followed you for so long. Without you..."

"I'm not abandoning you," Lucifer interrupted. "I'll always be here if you truly need me. But I can't be the one to lead anymore. The time has come for me to step down."

The finality in his tone left no room for argument. Valyron, Leo, and Kael exchanged glances, the weight of the moment sinking in. Their leader, their friend, was leaving them. The realization hit harder than any blow they'd taken in battle.

After a long pause, Leo spoke, his voice soft but filled with understanding. "If this is what you truly want... we'll support you." Valyron nodded. "You've earned it, Lucifer. After everything... you deserve peace." Kael, though reluctant, finally agreed. "You've led us through countless battles. If anyone deserves to walk away from war, it's you." Lucifer's eyes softened with gratitude, but the guilt remained. "Thank you. I only hope... that by stepping down, I can finally do something right."

As they stood together in the quiet aftermath of the war, they knew this was the end of an era. Lucifer, the one who had been their beacon of strength, was laying down his sword. The future felt uncertain, but perhaps, for the first time in a long while, there was hope for something other than war.

"I'll stay for a while," Lucifer added, "help you transition, find someone who can take over... but after that, I'm gone." They nodded, accepting his decision, though the void he would leave in their lives would be immense. And so, the warrior who had once been the fiercest of them all had made his choice. He would seek peace, and in doing so, he hoped that the world, and those he left behind, could do the same.

Lucifer turned toward the horizon once more, feeling the weight lift slightly from his shoulders. He had made his decision. Now, it was time for the next chapter—one without war, one without violence. One where, finally, he could rest. For the first time in years, Lucifer smiled. He found joy between the guilt, on feeling the support of his friends.

A Few Hours Later

Lucifer called upon a meeting in his court inviting everyone, from the royal people to the villagers. Leo understood the agenda of the meeting and exclaimed with concern, "This kingdom needs you, Lucifer! You can't leave now, not when there is still hope to rebuild. The people look up to you, kids look up to you, and so do we. We find hope in you, a hope equivalent to trust. When all goes down, we know that you will step up and take the matters into your hand. Just like in this war."

Lucifer's gaze softened as he looked at Leo and said, "I know Leo, and I understand. You know me more than others, you have helped me, eradicate the dark side that used to run in me. And that's the reason! When I left my home, I had decided that I would do good for the community and not let my darkness control me. I took the oath that if.... if someday because of me, a community suffered, or my actions led to mass bloodshed, I would step down."

Kael concerned, also participated" Surely there is another way. You stepping down won't just erase all the threats." "I am fully aware of that fact but the longer I sit on this throne, the more violence prolongs." Lucifer stated. Valyron, always the one with measured words, stepped forward, "If not you, then who? Who will lead us into this next era? The people here also need an answer, and soon."

Leo, clenched his fists, the emotions boiling over, "But this isn't about us, Lucifer! This is about you. This kingdom is a reflection of who you are, of what you built. Without you, who will protect them when the next Kharon rises?" "That's where you come in, Leo. You are a mastermind, a leader who never gives up and fights until it isn't over. Valyron has always warned us before a big battle and I'm sure it will happen again. And Kael, a great warrior and a leader. I am pretty sure he will always be by your side when you need him. And it's not like I am abandoning you! When the time comes, when you will really need me, I will return."

And thus, Lucifer passed on the crown to Leo. The proclamation led with a huge chants and celebrations.

32

THE LEADER'S FAREWELL

Lucifer stood at the edge of the kingdom's courtyard, the evening sun casting golden hues across the land that had been his home for so long. His time as king had come to an end, but his duty was not over yet. Before he left, there was much to do.

Valyron, Leo, and Kael had gathered, their faces a mix of solemnity and determination. They knew the importance of this transition, and though Lucifer was stepping down, he had taken it upon himself to help them make the handover as smooth as possible.

The following weeks had been busy, with Lucifer guiding them through everything, from military structure to the intricacies of diplomacy. Together, they met with village leaders, soldiers, and scholars. Lucifer passed on every bit of wisdom he had, making sure that the kingdom would not falter under the weight of the change.

"I'll be here if you need advice," Lucifer reassured them after a particularly long meeting about the reorganization of the army. "But it's time for you to lead on your own."

Valyron nodded, his eyes reflecting the gratitude he felt. "We'll make you proud. This kingdom will remember your legacy forever."

Kael smiled, his usual stoic demeanour softening. "You've taught us well. But this will always be your home."

Leo stepped forward, his gaze fixed on Lucifer's. "It won't be the same without you. But we understand why you're doing this."

The Leader's Farewell

Lucifer placed a hand on Leo's shoulder. "This kingdom is in good hands. You three are more than capable."

The time had come. After days of preparations and farewells, Lucifer stood at the foot of the grand steps leading to the courtyard. His whistle echoed across the sky—a signal only one creature could respond to.

From the thin air above, the silhouette of Draco appeared, emerging from the clouds. The mighty dragon swooped down with grace, his dark wings outstretched, and landed before Lucifer, sending a gust of dust swirling into the air. Draco's eyes gleamed with an intelligence that matched his master's.

Lucifer stepped forward, his voice soft but firm. "I'm sorry, Draco. It's time for us to leave."

Draco tilted his massive head, a low rumble vibrating from deep within his throat. His sadness was palpable, even without words.

Valyron approached the dragon first, stroking the side of Draco's scaled face. "You've been a fierce companion, Draco. One of a kind," he said with a soft smile, his hand lingering for a moment longer. As he moved away, Draco gave a gentle lick to Valyron's arm—a final show of affection.

Leo followed next, his hand trailing across Draco's sleek, black scales. "We'll never forget you," Leo whispered. "Or you, Lucifer." Draco licked his hand, leaving Leo with a bittersweet smile.

Kael, always quiet in his affection, approached last. He placed his forehead gently against Draco's head, closing his eyes in a silent farewell. The connection between them was one of unspoken understanding, and Draco's rumble grew softer, as if acknowledging the bond.

But before Lucifer could leave, Valyron and Leo stepped forward once more, their faces lit with a glint of excitement. "Wait," Valyron said. "We have something for you."

Together, they led Lucifer to the centre of the courtyard. There, covered with a large cloth, was a towering figure—a surprise they had worked on for days.

The Fate of the Fallen

Valyron and Leo grinned at each other before pulling the cloth away to reveal the grand statue beneath.

It was breathtaking.

The statue depicted Lucifer in his most iconic stance—his sword drawn and held high above his head, his expression one of fierce determination and strength. By his side stood Draco, wings spread wide, a mirror image of his real counterpart. The detail was extraordinary, from the sharp angles of Draco's wings to the intricate etchings on Lucifer's armour. Every scale on Draco's body was captured, and even the glint of resolve in Lucifer's eyes was immortalized in the stone.

Lucifer stood in awe, speechless. The statue was taller than any man, towering over the courtyard, a symbol of his leadership and the bond he shared with Draco. It was the kind of monument that would stand for centuries—a reminder of the king who had fought for peace and the dragon who had stood by his side through it all.

"Do you like it?" Leo asked, a hint of nervousness in his voice.

Lucifer blinked, his throat tightening with emotion. "It's... perfect. Thank you."

They stood there for a moment, the statue casting long shadows across the courtyard, a fitting tribute to a king and his faithful dragon. But now, it was time.

Lucifer mounted Draco, taking one last look at the kingdom he had built. He nodded to his friends—his brothers—and with a soft command, Draco lifted into the sky. The wind whipped around them as they soared higher and higher, leaving the kingdom behind.

For hours they flew, crossing valleys and mountains, until the sprawling landscape gave way to the ocean. Far away from any known lands, on a small, remote island, Lucifer and Draco landed. This was where Lucifer would begin his new life.

The Leader's Farewell

The island was lush with greenery, surrounded by calm, crystal-clear waters. A small beach stretched along the shoreline, perfect for Draco to rest by the sea. Here, there would be no wars, no battles—just peace. Lucifer set to work, building a modest wooden bungalow near the water's edge. It wasn't grand, but it was enough to rest at least for a few weeks. A small garden lay beside it, and using the resources around him, Lucifer crafted a simple machine made of wood, harnessing the water's natural flow to generate electricity.

As the sun began to set, Lucifer sat on the porch of his new home, watching the waves lap against the shore. Draco curled up nearby, his great body rising and falling with each breath. For the first time in what felt like an eternity, Lucifer felt at peace.

The stars began to dot the sky, and Lucifer looked up at them, and saw that the constellation looked like the faces of Valyron, Leo, and Kael. They were strong. The kingdom was in good hands. He had done all he could for them.

Lucifer leaned back, closing his eyes. The future was no longer his to shape. But for the first time in years, he was ready to embrace the unknown. He had earned his peace.

And so, on the quiet shores of a distant island, the king who had once led armies into battle, who had fought for peace and justice, finally found his own.

33

BETWEEN THE WAVES AND STARS

Lucifer had spent many weeks on the island, enjoying the peace and quiet after years of war. His days were spent constructing and perfecting his humble beachside home, but even with the tranquil surroundings, there was a restlessness building inside him. The isolation, once a relief, had started to wear on him. Draco, his loyal dragon, had flown away to explore distant lands, leaving Lucifer with only the sound of waves and the rustling of palm trees to keep him company.

One late afternoon, while Lucifer sat by the shore, his thoughts drifting like the waves, something unusual caught his attention. In the distance, through the hazy sunset, he spotted a small boat making its way toward the island. His instincts sharpened instantly—no one knew of this place, and it was too remote for casual travellers.

As the boat came closer, Lucifer could make out a figure standing on its deck, accompanied by a peculiar creature. Its sleek fur glistened in the dying light of the sun, and as it stepped onto the island with its owner, Lucifer could see it was unlike any animal he had ever encountered. The creature stood about waist-high, with a body covered in thick, shimmering black fur. It had the general shape of a feline, but its tail split into three at the end, each tail tip glowing faintly in the dimming sunlight. Its eyes were a striking gold, glowing faintly as if lit from within, and its paws left small, crackling sparks of electricity wherever they touched the ground. The creature exuded both elegance and danger, walking beside its master with quiet confidence.

Lucifer observed the man, who seemed equally surprised to see someone on the island. He was tall and lean, his clothes worn but clean, suggesting he had been traveling for some time. There was an air of intelligence about him, a sharpness in his eyes that told Lucifer this was no mere wanderer. Slung over his shoulder was a large bag, brimming with various tools and gadgets, clearly marking him as someone who dealt with technology and engineering. Around his neck hung a chain with a small, engraved badge.

Lucifer stepped forward cautiously but didn't reach for his sword. There was no need for violence, not yet at least. "Who are you?" Lucifer called out, his voice steady but firm.

The man raised his hand as if to show he meant no harm, but his pet, the creature with the glowing tails, growled softly, its three tails whipping in the air like charged whips. "Easy, Kivros," the man muttered. "Oh, and this right here is my companion.... He is a hybrid of a wolf and a dragon" introducing the creature, who obediently lowered its head but kept its gaze locked on Lucifer.

"I could ask you the same," the man replied, his voice calm. "I wasn't expecting to find anyone here."

Lucifer's eyes narrowed slightly, scanning the stranger. He noticed the chain around the man's neck, more specifically the badge hanging from it. It was a symbol he recognized—a marking from a village not too far from his own kingdom. "That badge," Lucifer said, pointing. "You're from the village nearby?"

The man glanced down at the badge as if he'd forgotten it was there. "Yes, I am," he replied, adjusting it. "Not many know of that place, though. You seem familiar with it."

Lucifer stepped closer, feeling the tension begin to ease. "I used to rule over a nearby kingdom," he said, his tone softening. "But that was a long time ago. Now, I've come here seeking peace. But you…what brings you to this island?"

The man hesitated for a moment, then extended his hand. "I'm Elyon," he introduced himself. "And this is Kivros, my companion." The creature, sensing the calm, stopped its low growling and observed Lucifer with curious, glowing eyes.

Lucifer shook Elyon's hand, feeling the firm grip of someone who had travelled far and seen much. "Lucifer," he replied simply, deciding to omit his past titles for now. "What brings you here, Elyon?"

Elyon gave a half-smile. "I've been wandering for some time, looking for a place to settle. I'm something of a builder and inventor. My village was destroyed years ago, and since then, I've been searching for somewhere to start anew. I came across this island by chance."

Lucifer's curiosity grew. "A builder and an inventor?" he echoed. "You must have many skills then. What are you building out here in the middle of nowhere?"

Elyon gestured to the bag slung over his shoulder. "Tools and gadgets mostly. I specialize in creating machines that can help advance a village—water filtration systems, wind turbines, things like that. In fact," he said, a flicker of excitement lighting his eyes, "I was planning to find a suitable place to start some new projects. Maybe help a nearby village advance its infrastructure."

Lucifer studied him for a moment, impressed by the man's ambitions. "You've come to the right place then. This island is peaceful, but it's also isolated. I could use someone like you to help build and advance things around here."

Elyon tilted his head, intrigued. "You mean…you're offering me a place to stay?"

Lucifer nodded. "I know how it feels to lose everything and search for a new beginning. If you need a place to work and stay, you're welcome to make this island your home for a while. I could use the company."

Elyon seemed taken aback for a moment, then a genuine smile spread across his face. "I appreciate the offer, Lucifer. It's been a long time since I've had a place to call home." He glanced at Kivros, who had now sat beside him, its three tails curled around its body, the faint electric hum fading. "And I think Kivros approves too."

Lucifer chuckled, feeling a sense of relief at the prospect of not being alone anymore. "Then it's settled. Come, I'll show you the place I've built. It's not much, but it's sturdy, and there's plenty of room for your work."

As the two men walked toward the wooden house Lucifer had built, a sense of camaraderie began to form between them. Elyon's technical expertise and Lucifer's strategic mind seemed to complement one another in unexpected ways. They talked about the future, about plans for advancing the island and possibly helping nearby villages rebuild.

Later that evening, as they sat by the fire outside the house, Elyon asked, "So, Lucifer, why did you leave your kingdom behind? You don't strike me as the type to abandon everything so easily."

Lucifer gazed into the flames, the memories of past wars and battles flashing through his mind. "I didn't abandon them," he said quietly. "I retired. After everything I went through, I needed peace. And I needed to be away from the chaos, from the destruction…from the person I had become."

Elyon nodded, understanding the weight behind those words. "I see. Sometimes, stepping away is the only way to find yourself again."

Lucifer glanced at Elyon and smiled faintly. "Maybe. But for now, I think we both have a chance to build something new here. Something better." No sooner did they stop talking than Draco came back from exploring nearby land. Lucifer looked at him wholeheartedly," Oh how I have missed you, Draco! Well, it's nice that you came because we have new companions with us, new friends: Elyon and Kivros."

Elyon waved his hands to the big black dragon. While Draco still didn't know completely who they were, trusted Lucifer and let out a roar, a message to his new friends that they are welcome.

Elyon raised his cup, a silent toast to new beginnings, as Kivros purred softly at his feet. The night was quiet, but for the first time in a long while, Lucifer didn't feel alone. And as the stars twinkled above, he realized that perhaps this island wasn't just a place to escape—but a place to rebuild, not only his life but also the lives of others.

34

A BOND FORGED IN SOLITUDE

The sky above was streaked with hues of dusk as Lucifer sat at the edge of the shore, his gaze drifting across the endless horizon. The waves lapped rhythmically against the sand, their whispering, steady rhythm a comfort he'd come to know in these secluded days. Sitting here, in the stillness of evening, Lucifer felt more at peace than he'd ever known—and yet, the weight of his past still lingered, like a shadow cast by the dimming light.

Nearby, Elyon approached quietly, his companion Kivros trotting beside him. Kivros was unlike any creature Lucifer had seen before. His coat was sleek and dark, catching the fading light in a way that made him appear almost ethereal. His eyes glowed with a sharp intelligence, and his long ears twitched as he took in every sound, constantly alert. Lucifer watched as Elyon settled beside him, the two men exchanging a nod, while Kivros stretched out, laying his head on Elyon's knee, loyal and calm.

Breaking the comfortable silence, Elyon spoke, his voice low but steady. "You ever wonder if there's something more out there? Beyond all the battles, beyond the kingdoms and endless power struggles… maybe something closer to a real life, one that isn't shaped by war?"

Lucifer felt a faint smile tugging at his lips, though it didn't quite reach his eyes. "There was a time when I dreamed of something like that. Back when I thought peace was within reach." He paused, staring out into the open sea. "But fate has its own ideas, and I've always been pulled back. Even now, after leaving everything behind, I'm learning what it means to be… just myself. Strange, isn't it?"

Elyon nodded, a hint of sadness in his gaze. "Sometimes, the strongest among us end up feeling the loneliest. We build walls, we armour ourselves, and somewhere along the way, we forget what it's like to truly belong, to just be."

They sat in silence, the only sounds the soft rustle of the waves and the occasional distant cry of a seabird. Kivros, ever alert, chased after a crab that scuttled across the sand, his agile body moving in quick, precise motions. Elyon chuckled at his pet's antics, and the two men exchanged a glance, sharing a quiet understanding.

As the evening deepened, Elyon shared stories of his own past—of a quiet village where he once lived, of friends who left to seek glory and adventure, of his own choice to leave in search of something greater. It was that same need for a deeper calling that had eventually led him here, to this remote shore, where he had crossed paths with Lucifer.

Lucifer chuckled as Elyon recounted a particularly amusing story of Kivros' loyalty. "So, you're telling me he scared off an entire gang of bandits with that howl?" he asked, reaching over to rub Kivros' head. The creature leaned into his touch, his eyes half-closed in contentment.

"Oh, he's full of surprises," Elyon replied, grinning. "People underestimate him because of his size, but he's got a heart as fierce as any warrior."

By now, the sky was a tapestry of stars, the faint light of the fire they had built casting warm shadows across the sand. At one point, Elyon turned to Lucifer, his expression contemplative. "Do you think about going back? To the kingdom, to the people you led?"

Lucifer hesitated, his gaze still fixed on the fire. "I don't think they need me anymore, not the way they used to. They need someone... new. Someone who can offer them a different path." He glanced at Elyon, his eyes thoughtful. "Maybe someone like you."

Elyon looked taken aback, his brows knitting in surprise. "Me? I've never led anyone in my life. I'm just... someone who's been looking for a place to belong."

Lucifer's voice was gentle but firm. "That's how it started for me too. Leadership isn't always about grand gestures or titles. Sometimes it's just about being there when others need you most." He placed a reassuring hand on Elyon's shoulder, his touch grounding and steady. "Don't underestimate yourself."

For a moment, they sat in reflective silence, the words hanging in the air between them. Elyon looked down, his face shadowed by thought, and Lucifer knew he'd planted a seed, a possibility Elyon hadn't considered before.

As dawn neared, they found themselves sparring, the soft sand beneath them adding a challenging layer to their movements. Lucifer was surprised by Elyon's skill; his moves were sharp and precise, and though he lacked the raw power Lucifer was accustomed to, his agility was unmatched. Watching him, Lucifer felt a flicker of respect and admiration, recognizing a warrior's spirit in this quiet man.

After an hour of practice, they both sat down, catching their breath. Elyon stretched, wincing slightly as he rolled his shoulders. "Not bad, for an old soldier," he teased, a playful glint in his eye.

Lucifer smirked, swatting him lightly on the back. "You're not so bad yourself, for a 'lost wanderer.'"

They both laughed, a sound that echoed across the beach, light and free.

As the sun finally rose, casting a warm glow across the landscape, Elyon turned to Lucifer, his face serious once more. "Lucifer... thank you. For everything. I didn't expect to find this kind of companionship, especially not here. It's... it's good to know I'm not alone."

Lucifer nodded, his voice barely above a whisper. "None of us should have to be alone."

With that, they sat side by side, watching the sun climb higher, filling the world with light and hope.

35

THE SPARK OF INNOVATION

As the dust had settled from recent battles, the kingdom was slowly finding its footing again. Valyron, Leo, and the rest had managed to restore order, but they knew that maintaining the peace meant more than just wielding swords—it required progress. That's when a stranger arrived at the kingdom's gates.

He wasn't a warrior, nor did he carry the demeanour of a noble. This man's hands were calloused from work, and his clothes were simple yet stained with soot and grease. He brought with him strange blueprints, sheets filled with sketches of machines and ideas that the kingdom had never seen before.

Valyron watched from the castle's balcony as the stranger was escorted inside. The people in the streets stopped to stare at the young man who was flanked by two guards. News had spread quickly—a skilled inventor had arrived, and with him, perhaps a way to change the future of the kingdom.

"His name is Orin," the guard announced, leading the man before Valyron. "He comes from the northern territories."

Orin wasted no time in laying out his plans. He unrolled his blueprints on the long oak table in the castle's meeting hall, explaining each drawing with an enthusiasm that was contagious. There were designs for windmills that would bring water from deep underground, a communication device that could carry sound over long distances, and sketches of a bridge that could withstand the strongest of storms.

Valyron was sceptical. The kingdom's traditions ran deep, and such radical changes could face resistance. But Orin's eyes burned with conviction, and as he spoke, it became clear that he wasn't just interested in new inventions—he wanted to give the kingdom a future free from the burdens of the past.

A few months went by as the village flourished with the help of Orin's inventions. The villagers trusted the new arrival now. They were happy and thus Orin gained Valyron and Leo's trust.

Lucifer sat by the fire, his thoughts drifting as Elyon spoke beside him. Their journey had been long, and though their destination remained uncertain, he found solace in the presence of his newfound ally. The quiet night was interrupted by the distant sound of hooves approaching. A messenger, clad in familiar armour, dismounted swiftly and handed Lucifer a sealed letter.

Lucifer broke the seal and scanned the message. The letter read:

"Lucifer,

The village is thriving, but challenges remain. We have stabilized things, but your guidance is needed now more than ever. A new citizen, Orin's innovations are shaping the community, and there is much more to build. Come back—we have work to do.

Valyron & Leo"

It was from Valyron and Leo—an invitation to return to the village. They had made progress, and they needed him there. A smirk tugged at his lips as he handed the letter to Elyon. "Looks like we're going back. Will you accompany me?"

Elyon read the letter and nodded. "Wouldn't miss it. Let's see what they've built."

"Alright," added Lucifer. "We will depart tomorrow"

The morning sun rose over the secluded island, casting long shadows over the heads of Lucifer and Orin. They were ready to leave. Draco, standing besides them was excited as he got to come back to the village he truly loved.

The Spark of Innovation

Valyron and Leo were waiting near the village gates when Lucifer and Elyon arrived. The sight of their old friend brought a relieved smile to their faces.

"Lucifer, it's good to see you back," Valyron said, clasping his shoulder. "Much has changed, and there's someone you should meet."

He gestured to a man standing nearby, his hands smudged with grease, a tool belt fastened around his waist. "This is Orin. His expertise in mechanics has played a huge role in improving the village."

Lucifer studied Orin, sensing his keen intellect and unwavering enthusiasm. "I appreciate anyone working to build something meaningful here," he said, offering a nod of acknowledgment.

Elyon stepped forward. "And this is Elyon," Lucifer continued. "A skilled warrior and a trusted companion."

Valyron raised a curious brow but simply extended a hand. "Anyone Lucifer trusts is welcome here."

The village was changing, slowly but surely. What had once been a collection of scattered huts and worn-down roads was now transforming into something more structured, more alive. Lucifer had always envisioned progress, but now, with Valyron and Leo ensuring stability, and Orin introducing innovation, that vision was finally taking shape.

Among them, Orin stood out. His passion for mechanics and innovation was contagious, and the village had begun to reflect his influence. From sturdy wooden carts with reinforced wheels to wind-powered grain mills, his ideas were not just ambitious—they were practical.

But the most striking addition was the clock tower. Towering over the village square, its gears and pulleys were a marvel of craftsmanship, built not just as a timepiece but as a symbol of the village's advancement. The project had been no small feat. Orin had worked tirelessly with blacksmiths, carpenters, and glassmakers, each component coming together like a well-tuned mechanism. The people watched in awe as the hands of the clock began to move, marking a new era.

Lucifer observed the progress with quiet satisfaction. While he had been sceptical at first, he couldn't deny that Orin's work was invaluable. Even the villagers, who had once hesitated to embrace change, were now engaged in the transformation. Some helped in construction, while others learned the workings of new machinery, eager to adapt.

"Things are shaping up well," Orin remarked in the evening as he adjusted the gears on the clock face. "But there's still much to be done."

Lucifer nodded. "It's not just about structures. The people need more—more security, better resources."

Orin wiped the sweat from his brow and grinned. "I've been thinking about that. If we can improve how resources are managed, especially something as vital as water, we could make life easier for everyone."

Lucifer raised a brow. "What do you have in mind?"

Orin didn't answer immediately, his mind already racing through possibilities. "I'll need some time to draft a proper plan," he said eventually. "But I believe we can create a system that ensures water reaches even the farthest homes without the daily struggle of carrying buckets from the well."

Lucifer considered the idea. It was ambitious, but so was everything Orin had proposed so far. And if there was one thing he had learned, it was that ambition—when paired with determination—could shape the future.

The village's transformation was far from over, but for the first time in a long while, it felt like they were building something that would last for a long time.

36

BLUEPRINTS OF HOPE

Life had started to move forward again. The weight of the war was slowly giving way to a new chapter—one focused on rebuilding what had been broken and making something better from the ashes. Leo, Valyron, and Kael, now at the helm, were working tirelessly to reshape the kingdom into a place of hope rather than fear.

Lucifer and Elyon wanted to have a better look and understand the changes brought by Orin. Valyron thought it was a great idea to show them the inventions properly. However, it was already dark. It made sense that they rest after their long travel.

The next day, as the sun rose over the castle walls, casting long shadows across the cobblestone streets, Orin, Elyon and the trio went on to see the machineries. First, they went to the marketplace.

"First up, the marketplace. Trade is very important if you need a stable economy. A stable economy can help in a lot of ways including military. Since the marketplace that has always been central to the kingdom's trade and culture, was battered by the war. Hence, I decided to renovate it."

A team of masons and carpenters had been assembled to clear the rubble and rebuild the foundations. Stone by stone, they had laid out the new marketplace, using designs that combined both traditional and innovative elements. There were wide, open spaces, where vendors could set up colourful tents instead of cramped stalls. Wooden awnings, carved with intricate patterns that celebrated the kingdom's history, would provide shade during the summer.

A sturdy stone fountain was built in the centre of the square, a place where people gathered to rest, trade stories, or simply enjoy the sound of water splashing down the carved steps. And, as they had looked before, the clock tower. Orin, with his love for machinery, had designed a towering structure that would house a mechanical clock, its gears and pulleys a marvel of craftsmanship. It was an ambitious project, that required metalworkers, carpenters, and a specialized glassmaker to craft the clock face. Months of effort culminated in the clock's installation. The clock's chimes echoed across the kingdom, marking the advancement of a place reborn from ashes.

As the marketplace flourished, attention turned to the kingdom's food supply. The war had left the soil scarred, and many farmers had lost their crops. Orin had proposed a solution that drew sceptical glances at first—greenhouses. It was an idea foreign to the villagers, who had always relied on open fields and good weather, but Orin had assured them it would work.

The greenhouses were simple: wooden frames covered with clear, treated glass that Orin's team produced in the smithies. They would provide shelter for crops, allowing farmers to grow vegetables year-round, safe from storms and frost. The design was sturdy and efficient, able to hold warmth in the winter and vent out excess heat in the summer.

They demonstrated how the sunlight could be captured and retained, how water could be collected and distributed through simple irrigation channels, and how even the smallest plants could flourish in the controlled environment.

By the end of the season, the first harvest was ready—ripe tomatoes, herbs, and other crops that had once struggled to survive now thrived in abundance. The villagers began to understand that progress didn't mean abandoning their traditions but improving them. New greenhouses sprang up across the countryside, each one a symbol of a future where the kingdom wouldn't just survive but prosper.

The final project that brought the kingdom into a new age was Orin's invention of oil lamps to light the streets at night. It was a simple idea but one that changed the way people lived. Before, darkness had brought fear and vulnerability, but now, the soft glow of light would be a constant companion, a reassurance that they were no longer living in the shadow of war.

Orin and Leo worked together to design the lamps—brass fixtures with glass shields to protect the flame from wind and rain. They set up lamp posts at intervals along the main roads and alleys, testing the placement to ensure that every corner of the kingdom would be illuminated.

The first night the lamps were lit was a celebration. Families came out of their homes to walk the streets together, marvelling at the warmth of the light. Children played games long after sunset, their laughter awake at night, alive and unafraid.

Witnessing Orin's advancements Lucifer was astonished. It had exceeded his expectations. He remarked, "You are a genius, young man! But there is still a slight problem. You have focused on problems regarding just economy and most of the people's needs. However, you missed on the most important one: safety."

Valyron and Leo added, "True! And the wells are also too far for people to transport water. How about we build an irrigation system that not only ensures safety of the kingdom but also help in irrigating the fields."

Orin smiled as a challenge laid upon him. "Alright, I need to think. But the challenge is accepted. Call upon a meeting in the council hall in an hour."

The council hall was filled with heated discussion. A blueprint was spread across the heavy oak table, revealing Orin's vision for the kingdom's future. He had arrived months earlier with wild ideas, and now his vision was starting to take shape.

"I've seen what works," Orin said passionately, leaning over the plans. "And I've seen what fails. If we want to move forward, we need to think beyond just rebuilding what we had. We need to create something new—something that stands the test of time."

"I show in front of you a blueprint of a water-powered mill, designed to make grinding grain and producing flour more efficient than ever before. The nearby river, which had once been used only for fishing and washing, would now be harnessed for the good of the entire kingdom."

He asked everyone to follow him so he could explain better. The villagers gathered along the riverbank, curious but hesitant, as Orin began to outline his plan.

He explained how a wooden waterwheel would be constructed, using beams of oak and pine harvested from the nearby forests. The wheel would be anchored with iron nails from the kingdom's blacksmith, its broad paddles designed to catch the force of the river's current. As the wheel turned, it would drive a set of heavy grinding stones inside the mill, making the tedious work of hand-milling grain a thing of the past.

The project became a community effort. Men and women worked side by side, hauling wood, shaping beams, and carving the paddles for the wheel. Leo, always one to lead by example, took up the axe alongside the villagers, his strength and dedication inspiring others to push harder. Valyron, his keen eye for detail, oversaw the construction of the mill's foundation, ensuring that it would withstand both floods and storms.

When the wheel was finally set in place, the entire village gathered to watch the first test. The wheel turned slowly at first, creaking and groaning as the river's current caught its paddles. Then it gained momentum, the rhythmic splash of water filling the air. Cheers erupted as the stones began to turn, grain pouring into sacks as the first batch of flour was produced—clean, fine, and effortless. It was a small victory, but one that marked the beginning of a new era.

37

THE GRAND FIESTA

The village was no longer just a settlement—it was a home. With the recent changes, the people had found a sense of belonging. The air was filled with the sounds of laughter, clinking tools, and occasional bursts of cheering as projects neared completion. But tonight was different. Tonight was not about work. It was about bonding.

Lucifer sat near the village square, his eyes warm as he watched villagers gathering in small groups, sharing stories, breaking bread, and enjoying the warmth of a well-earned rest. Nearby, Elyon leaned casually against a wooden post, his sharp gaze drifting over the crowd.

"You're thinking too much," Lucifer remarked with a playful smirk.

Elyon rolled his eyes. "I'm always thinking."

"Then tonight, let's try not to think at all. No strategies, no battles—just people enjoying the moment," Lucifer said.

A few yards away, Leo was engaged in a friendly duel with one of the village's younger lads. The boy, gripping his wooden practice sword, lunged at Leo, but the seasoned fighter easily sidestepped, lightly tapping the boy's shoulder. "Too slow," Leo teased. "Again!"

The young fighter's face crinkled with frustration as he turned to Valyron, who had been watching from the sidelines. "You'll never win like that," Valyron called out. "You need to anticipate."

"But how?" the boy asked, voice tinged with exasperation.

Valyron crouched beside him, speaking in a low, encouraging tone. "Watch his feet more than his sword. He's quick, so don't wait for him to strike—try to predict where he'll move next. Use your size as an advantage." He grinned and added, "Though, aren't you a bit small for swordfights?"

The boy's eyes sparkled with determination. "I may be small, but I'll grow stronger... just like The King."

Valyron laughed heartily, standing up and ruffling the boy's hair. "That's the spirit. Now go show him what you're made of."

As dusk deepened into night, the villagers lit a grand bonfire in the centre of the square. Its warm glow danced across weathered faces, and stories of old—of battles, lost loves, and hard-won victories—filled the air with hope and nostalgia.

At one point, Orin excused himself from the main gathering and slipped away to a quieter corner of the square. Elyon, noticing his retreat, followed after a moment of hesitation. Away from the boisterous celebration, they stood beneath the soft flicker of the firelight, the distant laughter of the villagers a gentle hum behind them.

"You've done well here," Elyon murmured quietly, his voice low and sincere.

Orin's eyes lit up with a touch of mischief. "Coming from you, that almost sounds like a compliment."

Elyon crossed his arms and shot him a half-smile. "Don't get used to it. Nice work... brother."

Orin's smile faltered just for a second before he quickly recovered. "Didn't expect you to say it out loud," he replied.

"Neither did I," Elyon admitted, and for a brief moment, the bond between them was palpable—a secret shared in the quiet amid the celebration.

Returning to the festivities, the villagers gradually began an impromptu dance. Couples paired up, children twirled, and even the more reserved elders couldn't resist tapping their feet to the rhythm of an old, soulful melody played on a well-worn stringed instrument. The music, gentle yet stirring, spoke of journeys and dreams, of hope reborn.

Leo, his face flushed from the friendly competitions, raised his mug of ale high. "To what we've built!"

"To what we've built!" the villagers echoed in unison, their voices rising in a jubilant chorus that filled the night.

Amid the revelry, laughter, and dancing, Orin suddenly straightened and clapped his hands. "Wait, I have an idea!" he announced, drawing curious glances.

Lucifer feigned exasperation. "Orin, it's a celebration. If you're about to say 'mechanics' right now, I might just throw you into that fire," he joked, prompting an eruption of laughter from the crowd.

From another corner of the square, a group of villagers organized a playful contest of strength and agility. Participants challenged each other to lift heavy stones, race across the open space, and even engage in mock wrestling matches. In one such bout, a villager boasted, "I bet you ten silver coins I can knock Leo down!"

Valyron, watching the scene with amusement, laughed. "You'll lose that bet," he declared.

The challenger squared off against Leo. As soon as the match began, Leo dodged the initial charge with a swift movement, sidestepped, and sent his opponent tumbling into a carefully arranged pile of hay. Cheers and laughter filled the air as the victor raised his arms in triumph.

"Anyone else?" Leo grinned, cracking his knuckles and inviting more challenges.

Elyon shook his head in amusement. "Reckless," he murmured, though his eyes sparkled with delight.

As the night deepened further, Lucifer found himself engaged in a quiet conversation with an elderly villager who had witnessed the village's darkest days. She spoke softly of battles fought long ago, of sacrifices made, and of the resilience that had carried them through. "You've given us something we never thought possible," she said, her voice trembling with emotion. "Not just safety, but a purpose—a reason to believe again."

Lucifer listened intently, nodding as her words settled deep in his heart.

The celebration stretched long into the early hours. But as the laughter continued, Elyon's gaze drifted toward the horizon, where the darkness of the night seemed heavier than before. A shadow of unease flickered across his face.

Orin noticed. "Something wrong?"

Elyon didn't respond immediately. His fingers absently traced the hilt of his blade as if feeling an invisible presence. "No… just a feeling." He forced a small smirk. "Probably nothing."

But as the festivities raged on, Lucifer caught the brief exchange and frowned slightly. For the first time that night, an unspoken thought lingered at the edges of his mind.

A storm was coming.

And this night of peace, however joyous, would not last forever.

38

FAITH AND FACADE

As the sun dipped below the horizon, a golden hue settled over the village, casting long shadows that stretched across the square where Lucifer, Elyon, Orin, Valyron, and Leo gathered. After the recent reunion and the excitement of seeing Orin's inventions, the group settled around a large stone table, ready to discuss the next chapter of their kingdom's story.

Orin unfurled a weathered piece of parchment on the table, revealing detailed blueprints and sketches. "This isn't just about defence," he began, tapping a sketch of a tower with a surrounding network of intricate lines. "If we build these watchtowers with early-warning mechanisms, the entire kingdom will be notified the moment any threat comes within range." He pointed to a set of symbols drawn in a pattern around the kingdom's border, each representing different aspects of the design.

Valyron studied the parchment with narrowed eyes. "A network of towers that signals danger? It's impressive, but how would they communicate?"

Orin leaned forward, enthusiasm radiating from him. "I've designed a system using mirrored lights and sound signals. Imagine—a watchman spots an intruder and uses a mirror to catch sunlight and send a beam to the next tower. At night, they'd use drums or a series of gongs. It's primitive but reliable. And with a little more work, I think we can make the system almost foolproof."

The group shared a thoughtful silence, contemplating the potential impact of such a structure. Finally, Leo spoke up, "This could change everything. We've always depended on word of mouth and messengers. This… this is immediate communication."

Lucifer, with his arms crossed, tilted his head thoughtfully. "But how would this help the people within our borders, those who aren't on the front lines?"

Orin smiled, his excitement mounting. "I thought about that, too. I've been experimenting with a water distribution system. If we dig canals and create reservoirs, water can reach the driest parts of the village. No more dragging buckets from far-off wells. Instead, water will flow directly to where it's needed."

Lucifer's eyes sparked with admiration. "A water system... That's incredible, Orin. Do you think it would be possible to set up irrigation for the crops, too?"

Orin nodded enthusiastically. "Exactly! I believe if we create a series of small, rotating water wheels and mills, it would save everyone so much time and labour. Crops would grow faster, and people could focus on other things, maybe even learning new trades."

Elyon, his pride evident, clapped Orin on the back. "You see, brother? You have a vision not just for protection but for prosperity. Our people will finally have the stability they deserve."

Valyron, ever the strategist, studied the designs with intensity. "Orin, what about defence? With water canals running through the village, aren't we creating weaknesses that intruders could exploit?"

Orin looked undeterred. "That's a fair point, Valyron. But I have ideas for that, too. We could design retractable gates over the canals or even small defensive towers at key points. If the enemy tries to use the waterways, they'll find themselves caught in a trap."

The others nodded, visibly impressed by Orin's foresight. There was an air of growing excitement among them as they realized the potential of Orin's plans.

Lucifer leaned forward, his gaze intense. "This is more than just survival, more than just defence. What we're talking about... is a new era for our people."

A deep silence fell over the group as they absorbed the weight of Lucifer's words. Finally, Leo spoke up, his voice filled with determination, "I'm all in.

We've spent so much time fighting for our lives that we never imagined what we could build. I say we focus our energy here—to make this kingdom a beacon of hope."

Valyron nodded, adding his support. "If we build these defence, it gives us something to protect that goes beyond ourselves. And if we can achieve prosperity… we will become a model for other villages."

Lucifer clasped Orin's shoulder firmly, his gratitude evident. "You've given us a vision of what we could be. And you, Valyron, Leo, Elyon—you're the heart of this new world we're building."

As they exchanged ideas, the group began brainstorming other possible advancements. Leo suggested creating a council that represented different parts of the village. "The people should have a voice," he said, leaning forward. "They should feel that they're part of this too. If we have representatives, it can help unify the kingdom."

Valyron agreed, adding, "And with everyone's input, we'll know where to direct our efforts. If farmers need support, they'll be heard. If the artisans need resources, we'll know. This isn't just for us; it's for everyone."

Elyon leaned back, his eyes alight with a vision forming in his mind. "Imagine schools… places where knowledge is passed down. Orin, maybe you could even teach others about technology and defence. We wouldn't just be a fortified kingdom. We'd be a place of learning and innovation."

Orin grinned, nodding eagerly. "Yes! With time, I could show others how to build, how to improve. It wouldn't just be me inventing. It would be a whole community."

The group grew animated, their energy feeding off one another as they spoke of their plans. By the time the meeting concluded, they had outlined a vision for the kingdom's future that extended beyond what any of them had previously imagined.

As they rose from the table, Lucifer looked out at the village with a sense of hope he hadn't felt in a long time. For the first time, he saw not just a place to defend but a home worth nurturing and growing. He placed a hand on each of their shoulders in turn, silently conveying his gratitude and pride.

"Tomorrow," Lucifer said, "we begin. We'll divide tasks, gather the people, and start building the foundation of our kingdom's future. And we do it together, for the good of everyone."

The group dispersed as the night deepened, each of them inspired, each carrying with them the conviction that they were on the brink of something monumental.

39

SHIFTING SHADOWS

The dawn sky cast a soft glow over the village, where the once-quiet mornings were now alive with sounds of construction and the hum of machinery. Villagers gathered in the square to watch the latest project take shape: a defence tower outfitted with new gears and early-warning systems Orin had introduced. Around them, a few children laughed, mimicking the movements of the workers, while older villagers murmured excitedly about how far their village had come.

Lucifer stood on the outskirts, his gaze sweeping over the bustling square. The sight filled him with a deep, quiet pride. His kingdom had transformed in ways he had only once imagined—and it wasn't just because of him.

"This," Leo said, stepping up beside him, "is something worth fighting for. Orin and Elyon have done wonders."

Lucifer nodded, his expression softened. "They have," he agreed, though there was a trace of something thoughtful in his voice. "They've given these people a new sense of hope. But sometimes, I wonder about their motivations… I can't shake the feeling that there's more going on beneath the surface."

Leo shot him a sidelong glance. "You think they're hiding something?"

Lucifer hesitated. "I don't know. But the way they exchange glances, the quiet conversations—they know each other more than they let on. I think it's wise to keep an eye out."

As if on cue, Elyon and Orin appeared at the far end of the square, conversing quietly with heads close together. Their words were lost in the buzz of activity, but the intensity in their eyes didn't escape Lucifer's notice.

At that moment, Orin caught their eyes and, with a broad smile, waved the crowd's attention to him. "Everyone, if I could have a moment!" His voice boomed over the crowd, drawing them in. "Today's progress belongs to all of you, to your hard work, and to the dreams we share of a safer future. I am but a humble tool of that vision!"

The villagers cheered, a few clapping Orin on the shoulder in gratitude. Elyon chuckled, patting Orin on the back. "There he goes again, playing the humble hero," he teased, though his grin was affectionate.

"Someone has to!" Orin replied with a wink. "But seriously, folks—this is only the beginning. We're not stopping here. You deserve walls that stand strong, lights that never go out, and a village that's safe from any threat."

Lucifer took a step forward, joining them. "You've done well, both of you," he acknowledged. "These people trust you—don't take that lightly."

Orin met his gaze, his smile unwavering but his eyes unreadable. "Of course not, Lucifer. You can count on us."

After the speech, the village erupted into celebration. Bonfires crackled in the evening air, and tables overflowed with food. As the laughter and music filled the square, Elyon found himself by Lucifer's side.

"Are you enjoying this, Lucifer?" Elyon asked, his gaze steady.

Lucifer gave a slight nod. "It's good to see them happy. Peace is… rare."

Elyon chuckled, "Rare indeed. Though I sometimes think you're restless here."

Lucifer's smile was faint, but his eyes held a glint of warmth. "Maybe a little. But I think I've fought enough for one lifetime."

Orin joined them, holding a goblet, his eyes shining. "We're grateful for everything you've done here, Lucifer. Truly."

Lucifer inclined his head in a quiet acknowledgment. "The fight was never just for me. It's for them, for every person who suffered under Kharon and the others."

Orin's gaze lingered on him a moment, contemplative. "Still, even leaders deserve peace."

Just then, Leo approached, pulling Lucifer aside. His tone was low. "There's something strange going on, Lucifer. I overheard Orin and Elyon talking about… a project. They didn't say much, but it seemed secretive."

Lucifer frowned, his earlier suspicions bubbling up. "Did they say anything specific?"

Leo shook his head. "Just bits and pieces. Orin mentioned 'advancement' and 'readiness.' It could be harmless… or something more."

Lucifer's eyes darkened as he scanned the square, watching Orin laugh easily with the villagers. "Let's keep this to ourselves for now," he decided, his voice a near-whisper. "We'll observe. If something's amiss, we'll know soon enough."

That night, as the fires burned low and the villagers drifted off to sleep, Orin and Elyon remained at the edge of the square, their voices hushed.

"This is the perfect opportunity," Orin murmured, his voice barely audible. "The people trust us. They'll follow our lead… if the time comes."

Elyon's face was a mask of determination. "Then we need to make sure everything is ready. Once we start, there's no turning back."

In the shadows, Lucifer and Leo exchanged a glance. Lucifer leaned closer to Leo, his voice low and guarded. "They're planning something, but what?"

Leo's jaw tightened, his eyes tracking Orin and Elyon as they moved quietly toward the far end of the village, where their newly constructed workshop stood. "It could be anything. Maybe they're looking to implement more advanced defence. Or maybe…"

"Or maybe they have a different agenda," Lucifer finished, a spark of concern glinting in his eyes. "Let's wait for the village to sleep, then we'll investigate."

Hours passed, the village now cloaked in silence under a starlit sky. Lucifer and Leo slipped from the shadows, making their way through the stillness toward

Orin's workshop. The building loomed tall, the faint glow of lanterns seeping through cracks in the wooden structure.

Lucifer gave a subtle nod to Leo, who pried open a side window, just wide enough for them to peer inside. The sight that met their eyes was far from what they'd expected.

Rows of intricate gadgets and devices lined the shelves, the tables filled with blueprints and tools unfamiliar to them. Maps of the kingdom, detailed and marked with strategic locations, were spread across one wall. In the corner, Elyon and Orin were hunched over a strange, metallic device emitting a soft, pulsating glow.

Elyon adjusted a dial, and Orin leaned in, his face a mask of concentration. "If we calibrate it properly, this device could channel an immense amount of energy," Orin murmured.

"And if we keep it contained until the right moment…" Elyon's voice trailed off, a hint of excitement flashing in his eyes. "Lucifer won't know what hit him."

At this, Lucifer's hand clenched, but he stayed silent. Leo's expression mirrored his disbelief and anger, but they knew it wasn't time to act. Not yet. They slipped back into the shadows, moving swiftly and silently back to the village outskirts.

Once they reached a safe distance, Leo's frustration finally broke through. "They're building weapons, Lucifer. They're going to turn on us, on everyone!"

Lucifer's face was grim, his gaze distant as he processed the revelation. "We were fools to trust them so completely. But now that we know their plan, we have the advantage."

Leo nodded, though his worry lingered. "But what's their endgame? Why go to all this trouble to gain our trust, only to betray it?"

Lucifer looked back toward the village, a mixture of sorrow and resolve hardening his expression. "Perhaps they want power, perhaps revenge… but whatever their reasons, they've made themselves clear. We need to be ready for when they make their move."

The following days were tense, a quiet unease settling over the village as Lucifer and Leo kept their suspicions hidden, watching for any further signs from Orin and Elyon. Lucifer worked alongside them in the village, never revealing what he'd seen, even as he felt Elyon's gaze linger a second too long, a trace of caution in his friend's usually warm smile.

At night, Lucifer strategized with Leo in secret, preparing for what he knew would be a difficult confrontation. He couldn't deny the pang of betrayal he felt, the heaviness that hung over him as he realized just how deep Elyon's deceit had run. This wasn't just a betrayal of trust—it was a betrayal of friendship, of everything they'd fought to build.

One evening, as the sky darkened, Orin approached Lucifer near the workshop. "Lucifer, we've made some progress on a few defensive measures," he said, his tone casual, but his eyes sharp. "Would you like to see them?"

Lucifer forced a smile, nodding. "Of course. I'm interested in seeing what you and Elyon have accomplished."

They walked to the workshop, where Elyon was waiting. He greeted Lucifer with a grin, motioning to the various devices laid out on the table. "Look at this," he said, gesturing to a mechanical sphere glowing faintly with a blue light. "It's a prototype energy source. Something new Orin and I have been developing."

Lucifer raised an eyebrow, maintaining his curious facade. "Impressive. And it works?"

Orin nodded eagerly. "Absolutely. It's just the beginning—we're on the verge of something groundbreaking. Imagine the possibilities, Lucifer… a world where we no longer fear the unknown."

Lucifer's gaze hardened, his expression unreadable. "Yes, I can see the appeal. But we need to remember what we're protecting here… the people, not just power."

Elyon's smile faltered, his gaze shifting. "Of course. This is all for them," he replied, though Lucifer sensed the slight edge in his voice.

Lucifer inclined his head, excusing himself soon after, leaving the workshop with a heavier heart. He met Leo back near the village's edge, his face shadowed with thought.

"They're planning something soon, Leo. Whatever they're building, it's nearly ready. We need to be ready as well," he said, his voice laced with determination.

Leo clenched his fists. "Let them try. They have no idea what they're up against."

As they slipped into the night, a silent promise settled between them. They would protect the kingdom, whatever it took—even if it meant confronting the friends who had once stood beside them.

40

THREADS OF TREACHERY

*I*n the quiet hours of early dawn, Lucifer and Leo found themselves on the outskirts of the village, discussing a plan. The weight of Elyon and Orin's apparent betrayal lingered heavily, like a silent storm gathering on the horizon.

"We can't keep avoiding the issue," Leo said, his voice taut. "If they're truly planning something dangerous, we need to be prepared to act—decisively."

Lucifer nodded, his face clouded with the same intensity that burned in Leo's. "I know, but if we act too soon, it could backfire. The villagers still trust them; they're seen as innovators. We'll need evidence if we're to warn the village without causing mass panic."

Just as they were deep in thought, a young villager approached them, breathless. "Lucifer! Leo! Orin and Elyon are holding a gathering in the village square."

Lucifer and Leo exchanged a quick glance, then hurried into the village. They arrived to find Orin and Elyon standing atop a raised platform, speaking to a gathered crowd. Orin's face glowed with a charismatic confidence, and Elyon was gesturing passionately as he spoke.

"Together, we have the power to advance this village beyond our wildest dreams," Elyon was saying, his voice carrying to the edges of the crowd. "We can move past old limitations, using new technologies to create security, prosperity, and power."

Orin nodded, addressing the crowd. "Imagine no longer fearing the wilds beyond our borders or the unknown threats that lie beyond. Imagine a world where our village is not just a place of refuge but a beacon of strength!"

The crowd murmured, captivated by their words. Lucifer felt a surge of frustration. Orin and Elyon were weaving a narrative that resonated with the villagers' fears and hopes, drawing them in with promises of safety and prosperity.

One of the older villagers raised a hand. "But what about the cost? What if this power brings danger? Should we not consider the risks?"

Elyon responded smoothly, "We have thought of everything. Each device, each strategy, has been crafted with your protection in mind. We seek only to defend this village."

Lucifer could feel the pull of Elyon's charisma, the almost hypnotic way he spoke, easing doubts and spreading his vision among the villagers. It was clear that they were manipulating the village, but he could see that the people didn't realize it.

When the gathering ended, Lucifer and Leo made their way back toward the workshop. They needed a plan, and fast.

Later that night, Lucifer and Leo worked on a countermeasure. They quietly gathered a few trusted villagers who had stood by Lucifer through thick and thin, including Kael, and shared their concerns.

"If Orin and Elyon are using technology to gain control over us, we need to level the field," Lucifer said. "If they intend to fight us with power, we must show them we aren't defenceless."

Kael, who had been watching Orin and Elyon's growing influence with concern, nodded. "I've been keeping track of their developments. If they're using energy sources and machines, there are ways we could disable or sabotage them if things go south."

Leo crossed his arms, contemplating their options. "We don't want a full confrontation if we can help it. But if they continue pushing, we'll have no choice."

One of the villagers stepped forward. "If it comes to that, we're with you, Lucifer. This village was built on trust and protection, not just power."

Lucifer's heart swelled with gratitude, and he nodded. "Thank you. Your support may make all the difference."

Days passed, and the tension in the village grew as Elyon and Orin continued their speeches, further entrenching their influence. Lucifer and Leo kept a close eye, quietly gathering evidence, waiting for the right moment to reveal the truth.

One evening, as the sun was setting, Orin approached Lucifer unexpectedly. "Lucifer," he said, his tone uncharacteristically formal. "Could I speak to you privately?"

Lucifer regarded him warily. "Of course."

Orin led him to the edge of the village, away from the prying eyes of the villagers. Once there, he turned, his expression serious. "I want you to understand, Lucifer, that what we're doing is for the good of the village. We're advancing them, giving them hope and security."

Lucifer's gaze was cold. "And at what cost? You're feeding them a dream that serves your ambition, not their safety."

Orin's face darkened. "Maybe you're too close-minded to see the potential here. This village could be a stronghold—an unbreakable force. But that won't happen if we keep living in fear."

Lucifer's voice was low but firm. "It sounds to me like you're building an army, not a home."

Orin sneered, taking a step back. "Believe what you want, Lucifer. But don't get in our way. We're building something that goes beyond you, beyond your outdated ideas of 'community.' "

With that, he turned and walked away, leaving Lucifer alone under the darkening sky, his mind racing. It was clear now that Orin and Elyon had no intention of backing down. They were moving ahead with their plans, regardless of the consequences.

Lucifer returned to Leo, his expression resolute. "They're going to escalate, and soon."

Leo nodded, his face equally grim. "Then we'll be ready. Whatever they throw at us, we'll be prepared to stand our ground."

Together, they began refining their plans, strengthening their alliances within the village, knowing that the moment of confrontation was drawing ever closer. They would need every ounce of strength and every ally to face the coming storm.

41

BENEATH THE SURFACE

The morning sun had barely risen, casting long, quiet shadows over the stone paths that wound through the kingdom. For the first time in weeks, the atmosphere felt oppressive—an undercurrent of tension that clung to the air. Lucifer stood outside his quarters, staring out across the training grounds. His mind was restless, a quiet unease settling into his chest.

"You look lost in thought, Lucifer." Valyron's voice broke through the silence, and Lucifer turned to see his trusted friend approaching. Valyron's expression was unreadable, but Lucifer knew him well enough to see the slight tension in his shoulders.

"I've been thinking," Lucifer began, his voice low. "Something feels… off. Ever since Elyon and Orin arrived, it's like there's something hanging in the air, a shift that I can't explain."

Valyron studied him closely. "You're not the only one who's noticed. Orin especially has been acting a little too… secretive. And Elyon, well, he's been distant. I don't trust them, Lucifer. Not completely."

Lucifer sighed deeply, running a hand through his hair. "I want to believe in them. They've fought alongside us, helped build this kingdom. But what if we're missing something? What if their loyalty isn't what it seems?"

"I've had the same doubts," Valyron said, his eyes narrowing. "I've seen Orin in the arsenal, working on something… something that doesn't belong in this kingdom. It's too advanced, too different. It's not the technology we've been using, Lucifer. It's like he's building something else."

The Fate of the Fallen

Lucifer's brow furrowed as he absorbed this. "What do you think he's doing?"

"I don't know yet," Valyron replied, his voice tense. "But I intend to find out."

Meanwhile, Elyon and Orin sat in the shadows of the castle's highest tower, hidden from the prying eyes of the others. Orin's fingers danced over a series of metal components, carefully piecing together a strange contraption. Elyon watched him with quiet anticipation, his gaze fixed on the device.

"It's almost finished," Orin said, his voice calm but filled with an edge of excitement. "Once we activate this, no one will be able to stop us."

Elyon nodded, his expression unreadable. "We need to be careful, Orin. Lucifer and the others… they trust us. If they find out…"

"Let them," Orin interrupted, his eyes flashing with determination. "The trust they place in us will make their downfall easier. Once we have control of the kingdom's defence, nothing will stand in our way."

Elyon's lips curled into a small, almost imperceptible smile. "And what about Lucifer? Will he be… a problem?"

Orin's eyes darkened. "Lucifer is the only one standing in our way. Once we've gained the trust of the people, once they see us as their protectors, he will no longer be needed."

Elyon's gaze lingered on the horizon, where the kingdom sprawled beneath the early morning light. A flicker of doubt crossed his mind, but he quickly pushed it aside. This was the path they had chosen—there was no turning back now.

The next few days passed with a strange tension hanging in the air. Orin and Elyon continued to work in secret, their conversations growing more cryptic and hushed. Lucifer, Leo, and Valyron, all busy with the kingdom's expansion, began to notice the subtle changes in their behaviour—Orin's late-night hours spent in the arsenal, Elyon's growing distance. But no one spoke of it outright, brushing it off as paranoia.

One evening, after a long day of overseeing the kingdom's construction projects, Lucifer sat alone in his study, the weight of the situation pressing down on him. He glanced over the reports from Valyron and Leo, the progress of the kingdom's new defence, and the plans for expansion. But something didn't sit right. He couldn't shake the feeling that something—someone—was conspiring against them.

A knock at the door startled him, and he looked up to see Leo standing in the doorway, his expression grave. "Lucifer, we need to talk."

"About what?" Lucifer asked, his tone more tense than he intended.

Leo stepped into the room and closed the door behind him, lowering his voice. "It's about Orin and Elyon. There's something going on, and I don't think we're seeing the full picture."

Lucifer leaned forward, narrowing his eyes. "What do you mean?"

"I've been watching them," Leo said quietly. "Orin, especially. He's been tinkering with devices in secret—things we don't even understand. And Elyon… He's been meeting with him late at night, away from the rest of us. I don't trust them, Lucifer. I don't trust Orin, and I'm starting to wonder about Elyon too."

Lucifer's heart sank, but he pushed the feeling down. "You're overreacting, Leo. They've been our allies."

"I hope you're right," Leo said. "But I'm starting to think we've been blinded by our own trust."

That night, Lucifer couldn't sleep. His mind raced with thoughts of Orin and Elyon, of the inventions and devices they had been building in secret. He tried to dismiss his doubts, but they wouldn't go away. He could feel the kingdom he had fought so hard to build slipping through his fingers.

In the dead of night, Lucifer slipped from his quarters and made his way to the arsenal. The corridors were silent, the castle's usual hustle and bustle replaced by an eerie stillness. He approached the door to the arsenal, his heart pounding in his chest. As he reached for the handle, he heard a sound from within—voices.

He hesitated, his hand lingering on the door. The voices were too quiet to make out, but they were unmistakably Elyon and Orin. He stood there for a moment, his pulse quickening, before he made his decision. Slowly, he pushed the door open.

Inside, Orin and Elyon stood over a table covered in strange, mechanical components. They didn't hear him approach, too absorbed in their work.

Lucifer stepped inside, his voice cold and firm. "What are you two doing?"

Startled, Elyon and Orin turned, their expressions quickly masking any trace of surprise. Orin's eyes flashed with a dangerous glint, and Elyon's lips curled into a smile that didn't quite reach his eyes.

"Lucifer," Orin said, his voice smooth but edged with something darker. "I didn't expect you to visit."

Elyon stepped forward, his gaze steady. "We've been… working on something for the kingdom, Lucifer. Something that will secure our future."

Lucifer's eyes narrowed. "I see. And what exactly are you building?"

"Something that will make us invincible," Orin replied, his tone almost too calm. "Something that will ensure no one can challenge our rule."

Lucifer's mind raced. The pieces were beginning to fall into place. He looked from Orin to Elyon, seeing the truth in their eyes but he just couldn't believe it. They weren't building to protect the kingdom—they were building to take it.

The weight of the thoughts of betrayal were eating him. The trust he had placed in them, the loyalty they had shown—everything was starting to fall out. He had been blinded.

But the betrayal wasn't complete yet. There was still time. Still time for him to be hurt the most.

"What exactly do you think you're doing?" Lucifer asked, his voice low and controlled, though the anger simmered beneath the surface.

Elyon's smile widened, his gaze unyielding. "The question, Lucifer, is not what we are doing, but what we will do next."

With the seeds of betrayal now planted, the kingdom stood at the edge of a precipice. Lucifer was worried, the path forward was unclear. Trust had been shattered, and once it was gone, there was no turning back.

42

BONDS BROKEN

Elyon and Orin moved swiftly through the shadows, their faces hidden beneath the hoods of their cloaks. They were silent, calculating. The village stretched out before them, unsuspecting, nestled in the darkness of the night. They had prepared for this moment. The traps were set. The villagers had no idea what was coming.

With practiced ease, Elyon signalled to Orin. They began to move, their footsteps light against the dirt. A few villagers, unsuspecting in their evening routines, crossed the path where a tripwire lay hidden in the grass. The first trap was sprung—a sharp snap echoed through the air, followed by a sickening thud as the wire jerked taut, sending the unfortunate man to the ground. He struggled, trying to break free, but the net closed around him, lifting him off the ground, leaving him hanging, helpless.

Elyon watched from the shadows, a cold glint in his eyes. Orin stepped forward, a wicked smile curling his lips as he drew a blade. The man screamed as Orin cut him down, the knife flashing in the moonlight before plunging into the victim's chest.

They moved to the next group, a family gathering firewood. Elyon and Orin had already placed several traps nearby, ensuring that every movement was a risk. The family didn't stand a chance. A loud snap echoed again, and another net shot out, tangling them. One by one, Elyon and Orin made their kills, methodical, without hesitation, as if they were simply carrying out a task. The children's screams were silenced in seconds, their small bodies falling limp to the dirt.

They continued their work, spreading terror through the village, one group at a time. Each trap they set, each life they took, was done with cold efficiency.

Their betrayal was complete. The villagers, who had once trusted them, now faced the cruel reality that their so-called saviours had become their executioners.

A man—bloodied, battered, and terrified—managed to escape the chaos. He ran blindly through the forest, his breath ragged, feet stumbling over roots and rocks. He pushed himself harder, the sounds of pursuit growing fainter, but the memory of the slaughter was fresh in his mind. His only thought was to reach the camp—to find Lucifer and tell him everything.

After what felt like an eternity, the man stumbled into Lucifer's camp, collapsing to his knees. His eyes were wide with fear, the weight of what he had witnessed still gripping him. Lucifer, Valyron, and Leo rushed to his side, pulling him up, but the man could barely speak, his breath shallow, his body trembling from the exertion and terror.

"They… they… they killed them…" the man gasped, his voice barely a whisper. He coughed violently before continuing. "Elyon… Orin… they… they slaughtered them all. Trapped us, one by one… like animals… children… gone."

Lucifer's heart dropped as the weight of the man's words hit him. The realization was sickening, but the truth was undeniable. Elyon and Orin had betrayed them all. They weren't just enemies now; they were murderers.

"Tell me everything," Lucifer said, his voice cold, his hands clenched into fists.

The man, still struggling to breathe, nodded. "They promised us freedom… but it was all lies. They… they set the traps, split us up into groups, killed us like we were nothing." He paused, shaking his head. "I couldn't stay… I ran as fast as I could…"

Lucifer stood, his face a mask of fury. Valyron and Leo exchanged grim looks, their faces reflecting the same disbelief and anger. The betrayal was complete, and the time for mercy was over.

Lucifer turned toward his allies, his voice dark with resolve. "Prepare yourselves. Our predictions have turned out to be correct. Our trust has been broken and souls have been lost. We find them and make them pay for each and every soul they have taken from us. They should suffer from the same pain."

43

THE HUNT BEGINS

Elyon and Orin arrived at the shelter just as night began to fall, the deep silence of the forest wrapping around them like a suffocating cloak. The structure was well hidden, a fortress of sorts, crafted from the surrounding trees and camouflage. They had built it with one thing in mind: Lucifer. They knew he would come. And now, with the blood of the innocents on their hands, the time for preparation had arrived.

Inside the shelter, Elyon paced, his mind racing. He had expected resistance, but not on this scale. The betrayal had been swift, calculated—but so was Lucifer. Elyon couldn't afford to underestimate him, not now. The plan had to be flawless if they were to survive.

Orin sat on a rough-hewn wooden chair, staring at the map laid out on the table before them. His eyes traced the lines, the various routes they could take. There was no easy way out of this. Elyon had made sure of it. But the attack on the village had been only the beginning—there was much more to accomplish if they were to win the war.

"They'll be coming for us," Elyon muttered, his voice filled with a mix of irritation and resolve. "And they'll be coming from every direction."

Orin didn't look up from the map. He already knew this. "Then we use that against them. We spread them thin, hit them where they least expect it. We can't face Lucifer's entire army head-on. But we don't have to."

Elyon paused. "I'm not asking for their mercy, Orin. I want to crush them. You very well know why we came here."

"You will," Orin replied coolly, his eyes narrowing. "But not by throwing our forces into an open fight. We need to hit fast, strike with precision, create fear.

Let them chase shadows, get them into the woods. Split them up. They'll be too disoriented to know where the real threat lies."

Elyon nodded, the idea taking root in his mind. "Then let's do it. We'll take control of the night. We'll control the forest, the fear, and the uncertainty. And we'll make sure Lucifer regrets crossing us."

Meanwhile, far to the north, south, east, and west, Lucifer's army spread like wildfire across the land, torches flaming high, cutting through the darkness of the night. He had sent them in every direction—north, south, east, west, and even the wild, untamed stretches between the four points. No stone would be left unturned, no path left unchecked.

The soldiers moved with precision, marching through the thick trees, their faces grim, their eyes fixed on the task at hand. The sound of marching boots blended with the crackle of torches and the rustling of leaves beneath their feet. There was no rest, no pause. Lucifer knew the stakes. Elyon and Orin had to be found, and every minute wasted brought them closer to slipping away.

Valyron and Leo led a separate contingent, their eyes scanning the woods as they moved swiftly through the thick forest, knowing they were on the right path. They had a clear goal now—no more games, no more negotiations. It was war, plain and simple.

Lucifer walked with them, though he led from the front, his eyes never leaving the forest before them. The weight of his decision to send his army in every direction bore down on him. He knew this strategy would create chaos, but it was the only way to flush Elyon and Orin out. The brothers had built their shelter, and it was time to force them into the open.

The scent of pine and earth filled the air as they marched forward. Lucifer's thoughts were clouded with the weight of the betrayal, but his resolve never wavered. He would not allow Elyon and Orin to tear apart what they had worked so hard to build. The soldiers, too, knew this fight was personal, the air thick with anticipation.

As they marched, Lucifer's mind went over the plans again. He couldn't afford mistakes. His army had to be swift, relentless. They couldn't let the brothers

The Hunt Begins

scatter into the night, disappear like ghosts. Every corner of the forest was a potential battleground, and Lucifer's men were prepared for it.

They had to find them. And they had to make it count.

44

INTO THE ABYSS

*I*n the dim light of their hidden shelter, Elyon and Orin moved with cold precision, preparing for the next phase of their plan. Their faces were set with the grim determination of men who had crossed a line they could never return from. Each knew the price of betrayal; they had made their choice, and there was no looking back.

"We're running out of time," Elyon muttered, glancing at the makeshift map spread across the table. "Lucifer's forces will be on us before sunrise."

Orin gave a slight nod and reached beneath the table, pulling out a sturdy wooden box with reinforced metal edges. "Then let's give them something they won't expect." He opened the box, revealing several pieces of handcrafted machinery—a strange, almost alien sight in a world bound by swords and spears.

Inside were sleek, compact guns with intricately carved metal casings, their surfaces polished to a deadly gleam. Elyon picked one up, testing its weight. The weapons were handmade, meticulously crafted to be light and easily concealed, but their power lay in the bullets they fired. Each bullet was tipped with a blade so fine it could slice through any armour worn by Lucifer's soldiers, designed specifically to exploit weaknesses in their defence.

Orin loaded one of the weapons, checking the mechanism with practiced care. "These aren't just tools," he said, his tone low but charged with a dark pride. "They're weapons of war, designed to turn the tide."

Elyon smiled, though there was no warmth in it. "Good. Let them feel what we're capable of."

Orin nodded, loading a second gun and passing it to Elyon. "We'll make them think twice about coming after us. And by the time they realize what we're armed with, it'll be too late."

Together, they strapped the weapons to their sides, the weight almost reassuring. The guns were their insurance, a guarantee that they would control the battlefield. This wasn't just about escaping or outwitting Lucifer's forces—it was about reshaping the rules of combat itself.

Meanwhile, outside, Lucifer's forces continued their relentless search through the forest, their torches casting eerie shadows across the trees. They were hunting their prey, unaware that the rules of engagement were about to change in ways they'd never expected.

As they closed in, the brothers took up positions, slipping through the trees with stealth honed over years. They were ready, their fingers steady on the cold metal of the weapons, knowing the moment of reckoning was near.

45

BOUND BY BLOODSHED

The forest had grown deathly silent, the usual sounds of wildlife replaced by the steady thud of boots and the distant glow of torchlight cutting through the dark. Lucifer's army moved with focused intensity, combing through every inch of the woods. They knew their targets were near, but none of them realized just how deadly this encounter was about to become.

Lucifer, leading the largest group, kept his gaze fixed ahead, his expression unyielding. The betrayal of Elyon and Orin had wounded him deeply, but he was determined to finish this. No one would undermine his kingdom and walk away unscathed.

As they advanced, Valyron walked closely beside him, his staff gripped tightly in one hand, ready for whatever lay ahead. "They know we're coming, Lucifer. This could be an ambush," he warned in a low voice.

"I know," Lucifer replied, his voice like stone. "But this ends tonight."

Just then, a figure burst from the underbrush. One of Lucifer's scouts stumbled forward, blood streaking down his face, his breaths ragged. "My Lord!" he gasped. "It's them… they have strange weapons. They're picking us off from a distance—armour's no use against it!"

Lucifer's eyes narrowed. "Strange weapons? Show me where?"

The scout pointed back toward the dense trees. "They've set up traps and ambush points along the way… a few soldiers went ahead, but—" he broke off, his face paling as he looked back the way he had come. "We didn't see them coming. They… they're using something that pierces through everything."

Lucifer exchanged a grim glance with Valyron, realization dawning. "So, they've turned to forbidden tools," he muttered. "They've crossed every line."

Deeper within the forest, Elyon and Orin crouched behind thick foliage, guns ready in hand. They watched as soldiers advanced, completely unaware of what awaited them. Elyon steadied his breath, lifting the gun to his shoulder and aligning his sight on an approaching soldier. The soft click as he pulled the trigger was followed by a sharp hiss as the bullet found its mark, slicing through the soldier's armour with ease.

Orin watched the soldier fall, satisfaction flashing across his face. "We're thinning their numbers," he murmured. "They won't stand a chance once they're all scattered."

Elyon smirked. "This is only the beginning. Let them come. They'll soon understand the consequences of following Lucifer."

Moving silently, they repositioned, slipping into a new ambush spot farther along the path. They left a trail of confusion and carnage in their wake, every shot taking down another of Lucifer's soldiers. Their tactics were ruthless, efficient, and unpredictable, and the forest was now their battlefield, a place they controlled with deadly precision.

Lucifer's patience was wearing thin as they continued their advance, but it was clear the brothers had the upper hand with these weapons. Every few paces, they would find fallen soldiers—some clutching wounds, others still, eyes open in shock. These were the men Lucifer had trained, trusted, and led. This was an insult he couldn't let go unanswered.

He raised his hand, signalling his troops to halt. "We're changing our approach," he announced, turning to Valyron. "They're striking from the shadows, using those weapons to pick us off. We need to draw them out."

Valyron nodded, his face set with grim determination. "What's the plan?"

"We'll send a decoy group forward to lure them in," Lucifer replied, scanning the trees. "Once they reveal their position, we'll close in from all sides."

He summoned a small group of soldiers to act as bait, knowing the danger but aware there was no other way to confront the brothers head-on. The soldiers moved ahead, torches held high, their steps deliberate as they played their part in the risky ruse.

Elyon watched the decoy soldiers' approach, a slow grin spreading across his face. "They're trying to draw us out."

Orin laughed softly. "Let them think they're clever. It won't matter in the end."

Elyon raised his gun, aiming carefully. "Let's show them what they're really up against."

As the first shots rang out, the true confrontation began. Lucifer and his forces, armed only with conventional weapons, faced off against Elyon and Orin, whose technology gave them an undeniable edge. But as the brothers fired into the crowd, Lucifer moved in, closing the distance. Each step was a calculated risk, but he would not retreat—not now.

And so, in the heart of the forest, the final stand took shape. Blood, metal, and betrayal mingled in the shadows, marking the beginning of a brutal end.

46

OLD VALOUR, NEW VICES

The forest air was heavy, tense, as Lucifer led his forces deeper into the heart of the woods. The torchlight flickered on the faces of his soldiers, illuminating determination and fear alike. They moved in silence, weapons at the ready, every man and woman knowing that this was not an ordinary battle. This was war—a clash that would mark the ultimate betrayal and, perhaps, their end.

Valyron walked close beside Lucifer, his grip tight around his staff, his eyes flickering with a steely resolve. "They'll have anticipated us by now," he murmured. "We can't underestimate what they're willing to do."

Lucifer's expression was cold, darkened by fury and sorrow. "They think they can hide behind weapons and shadows. They don't understand the strength of loyalty, Valyron. They'll regret ever believing we'd crumble so easily."

A soldier in the front paused, glancing back at Lucifer, waiting for a command. Lucifer met his gaze, giving a firm nod. "We push forward. Prepare yourselves for anything they might throw at us."

They pressed on, each step crunching underfoot in the silence of the forest. Then, from ahead, a faint rustling broke the stillness. One soldier pointed into the darkness, his voice low. "Something's there."

Lucifer held up a hand, signalling them to halt, and strained his eyes. In the faint glow, a figure stepped forward, barely visible, but clearly armoured.

"Elyon," Lucifer's voice was a deadly whisper.

Elyon stepped forward, a confident smirk playing at his lips, with Orin close behind. Both were heavily armed, but in their hands were the newly crafted, deadly firearms they had unleashed in the earlier ambush. Elyon lifted his weapon casually, aiming it in Lucifer's direction.

"I was wondering when you'd find us," Elyon said, his tone mocking. "Sending your soldiers out like hunting dogs, but all they've done is stumble into their own graves."

Lucifer's eyes narrowed. "You've turned against your own kingdom, betrayed those who stood by you. Why?"

Orin gave a short laugh, joining his brother's side. "Loyalty to a lost cause means nothing. We're not servants, Lucifer. We're leaders, visionaries. We'll build something far greater than what you could ever hope to achieve."

Valyron stepped forward, anger in his voice. "You think betrayal will lead to greatness? All you've done is stain your names with treachery!"

Orin rolled his eyes. "Such old-fashioned ideals, Valyron. Have you not learnt anything from the war you fought with Kharon. This world is changing. You either evolve with it or fall beneath it. We have risen with the help of Kharon. He knew we were special. But you, you killed him treacherously."

Without warning, Elyon raised his gun, aiming at one of the soldiers beside Lucifer, and fired. The soldier dropped instantly, his armour useless against the sharp, lethal bullet that tore through it. Chaos erupted as soldiers scrambled, raising shields, but it was no use—the brothers' weapons were too powerful, too precise.

Lucifer's face hardened, grief flashing briefly as he saw his soldier fall. He glanced at Valyron. "We hold nothing back. Fight with everything you have! This is the last stand!"

A fierce battle broke out as Lucifer's forces surged forward, charging the brothers. Elyon and Orin retreated, taking cover behind trees, their guns blazing in rapid succession. Each shot rang out, cutting through the ranks of soldiers who fought desperately to close the distance.

Valyron raised his staff, unleashing a burst of energy that crashed against a tree where Elyon had taken cover, splintering it with a powerful impact. Elyon ducked, firing back with a deadly accuracy that forced Valyron to retreat momentarily.

Lucifer charged, his sword drawn, slashing through the undergrowth as he pushed toward the brothers. Orin turned his gun on him, firing a volley of shots, each one narrowly missing as Lucifer twisted and turned, moving like a shadow through the trees. Finally, Lucifer closed the gap, his blade crashing against Orin's weapon with a sharp clang.

Orin staggered back, momentarily thrown off balance. Lucifer seized the chance, his voice low and filled with fury. "You want power, Orin? Let me show you what true power feels like."

He raised his hand, dark energy gathering around it, crackling with an intensity that made Orin's eyes widen in fear. But before Lucifer could strike, Elyon intervened, firing at Lucifer's arm and forcing him to release his grip.

Lucifer grimaced, blood trickling down his arm, but he didn't falter. He raised his sword once more, his eyes blazing with determination. "You may have your tricks and your new weapons, but this battle will be won with heart and loyalty, not betrayal."

Elyon scoffed, reloading his gun with a swift, practiced movement. "Heart and loyalty? Those are relics of a past we're leaving behind, Lucifer."

Lucifer lunged forward, catching Elyon off guard. Their weapons clashed, the sound of metal on metal ringing through the forest. Around them, the battle raged, soldiers fighting desperately against the brothers' deadly advantage. Each fallen comrade fuelled Lucifer's fury, driving him to fight harder, faster, without restraint.

Orin and Elyon exchanged a brief glance, something unspoken passing between them. In an instant, they both stepped back, disappearing into the shadows. Lucifer stilled, his senses heightened, his gaze scanning the darkness.

"They're regrouping," Valyron said, breathless but determined as he approached. "They'll keep retreating, using their weapons to thin our numbers."

"Then we won't give them a chance," Lucifer growled, his eyes blazing. "They want to tear us apart? We'll show them they've underestimated us."

With a signal to his remaining forces, Lucifer pressed forward, determined to bring this war to an end.

47

TIDES OF WAR

The battle raged on with unrelenting ferocity, the night air filled with the echoes of clashing steel and the staccato cracks of gunfire. The forest was a chaotic blend of shadows and firelight as Lucifer's forces pressed forward, determined to reclaim ground lost to Elyon and Orin's ambushes.

Lucifer moved through the battlefield with lethal precision, each swing of his blade cutting down those who dared stand in his path. Beside him, Valyron wielded his staff like a beacon in the dark, directing waves of energy to shield their troops from the brutal attacks. Together, they led their soldiers deeper into enemy territory, each step a testament to their unyielding loyalty and belief in their cause.

As they advanced, Leo caught up to Lucifer, his face shadowed but resolute. "We've managed to push them back in the southern front," he reported, breathless. "But Elyon's men are retaliating fiercely. They're moving further into the forest, likely regrouping for a stronger strike."

Lucifer's gaze turned cold. "They're hoping to draw us in, weaken us in waves," he murmured. "But we won't play by their rules. This is our land—they can't hide forever."

He raised his voice to address the troops. "Stay close, cover each other's backs, and push forward. They think they can outlast us, but they've underestimated our strength."

With a rallying cry, his forces surged forward, spreading through the dense undergrowth. The soldiers moved cautiously, aware that any moment could bring a new barrage of bullets or a deadly trap set by the brothers. Valyron, ever watchful, caught sight of strange metal contraptions concealed among the trees.

"They've rigged the forest," he muttered to Lucifer. "These traps are set to explode at any sign of movement."

Lucifer's jaw tightened, glancing at the dark shadows around them. "Then we adapt. We'll move through in small groups—take down their traps before they can use them against us."

Valyron and Leo were standing besides Lucifer. They could see the darkness spreading within Lucifer. Valyron warned him, "Lucifer! You need to calm down a little. I don't think their plan was to destroy the village. But, destroy you through it. They know your weakness, and their plan is working." Leo agreed.

Lucifer, ignoring the fact said, "I don't care anymore. This happened once with Kharon. It cannot happen again. "

He gestured to several soldiers, splitting them into teams to navigate the treacherous forest paths. With a careful eye, they disarmed one trap after another, inching closer to where Elyon and Orin were suspected to be hiding.

As they advanced, a shadow darted from the trees, moving so fast that it was nearly invisible. A soldier shouted, falling to the ground as a sharp bullet pierced his armour. Valyron's head snapped toward the source, his grip tightening on his staff.

"Orin," he said, recognizing the shadowy figure retreating back into the darkness.

Lucifer nodded, his eyes narrowing. "They're circling us, picking us off one by one. We need to draw them out into the open." He signalled to his troops. "Prepare to hold position. When they approach, we close in."

The soldiers formed a defensive ring, their torches casting long shadows across the ground. For several moments, there was silence, each warrior bracing for the assault. Then, as if on cue, gunfire erupted from the shadows, bullets whizzing through the air and striking their shields.

Orin and Elyon emerged, firing with deadly precision, but this time, they weren't alone. A group of their loyalists charged forward, armed with the same handcrafted firearms that had torn through Lucifer's ranks before.

The air filled with the sound of gunfire and clashing steel as Lucifer's forces fought against the brutal onslaught. Lucifer surged forward, his sword flashing in the firelight as he confronted Elyon. Their eyes met—a clash of fury and betrayal—and without a word, they attacked.

Elyon dodged Lucifer's strikes, countering with swift shots from his firearm. Each bullet ricocheted off Lucifer's armour, barely missing his exposed neck and arms. Elyon grinned, mocking. "You're slower than I remember, Lucifer. Maybe you've lost your edge."

Lucifer's gaze burned. "I may have lost allies, but I haven't lost the strength to finish what I started."

With a sudden surge of energy, Lucifer lunged, his blade catching Elyon off guard. The two wrestled for control, Elyon's gun clattering to the ground as he struggled against Lucifer's grip. Just as it seemed Lucifer had the upper hand, Orin appeared from behind, his own gun raised and aimed.

A warning shout from Valyron saved Lucifer in the nick of time. He twisted, dodging the bullet aimed for his back, but the distraction allowed Elyon to break free, shoving Lucifer backward.

Around them, the battle continued, brutal and unrelenting. Lucifer's forces fought valiantly, pushing forward even as more fell to the brothers' ruthless tactics. The forest floor was littered with fallen soldiers, and the smell of smoke filled the air.

But slowly, the tides began to shift. Valyron's magical barriers shielded their ranks, giving Lucifer's forces the edge they needed to close the distance. And as each trap was dismantled, the brothers' advantage lessened, leaving them vulnerable.

Finally, Orin and Elyon retreated further into the forest, their movements growing desperate. Lucifer, Valyron, and Leo followed, determined to end this betrayal once and for all. As they closed in, Lucifer's voice rang out, filled with conviction.

"This ends tonight. You betrayed everything you stood for, Elyon. Your power won't save you from justice."

Elyon sneered, backing up against a tree. "Justice? Don't delude yourself, Lucifer. There's no justice in a world where only the strongest survive."

Without hesitation, Lucifer raised his sword, preparing to strike the final blow. But Elyon grinned, a flicker of triumph in his eyes as he revealed a small detonator in his hand.

"We're not finished yet," he said, pressing the button.

A thunderous explosion rocked the ground, and fire erupted around them as Elyon and Orin escaped deeper into the shadows. Lucifer shielded himself from the blast, gritting his teeth as he watched the brothers disappear.

As the smoke cleared, Valyron and Leo approached, their faces grim. "They're not done fighting, but neither are we," Leo said, breathing heavily. "We can't let them regroup."

Lucifer's gaze was steely, his resolve unbroken. "We'll hunt them to the ends of the earth if we have to. Their betrayal will not be forgotten."

48

THE FIRE'S REACH

Lucifer stood at the edge of the forest, his eyes scanning the dark expanse. He knew they were close—he could feel it. Elyon and Orin were out there, hiding somewhere in the thick woods, but they couldn't run forever.

"Have you seen anything?" Leo asked, his voice low as he moved alongside Lucifer.

"Nothing," Lucifer replied, his gaze never leaving the shadows of the trees. "They've slipped into the forest, and the night hides them well. But we can't waste any more time searching the old way."

Valyron, who had been silently assessing the area, stepped forward. "We need to force them out," he said. "We know their tactics. They'll stay hidden until we're too exhausted to chase them."

Lucifer's lips curled into a grim smile. "Then we'll make sure they can't hide any longer."

Turning toward the rest of his troops, he raised his voice. "Prepare the trebuchet. We're going to flush them out."

Leo shot him a questioning look. "The trebuchet? You think that'll do the trick?"

Lucifer's eyes flicked back to the forest, his expression hard. "If they think they can hide in the dense woods, they're mistaken. They've underestimated the power of our reach."

The trebuchet, an enormous siege weapon that had been prepared earlier, was ready. It stood like a mechanical beast in the clearing, its giant arm poised for action. The soldiers quickly loaded massive boulders onto the sling, attaching fuses that would set them alight on impact.

"Light the fuses," Lucifer commanded.

Valyron was worried. He asked if he was sure about this.

The flames from the torches flared as the soldiers worked quickly, and Lucifer could feel the weight of every passing second. The night was growing colder, the flames casting long shadows across the field. It was a tense waiting game now—no one could afford to blink first.

"Engineering marvels were brought to us, bringing growth and prosperity. Good thing brought in by good people for the good of the people - little did we realised that evil laid somewhere hidden. Greed for power and wealth is driving them. Greed consumes them and they are consuming and destroying what was created by them. Earlier the evil was visible, today lies an evil hidden in the cloak of good. It's our duty to destroy it before it destroys the whole world. So reach forward and raise your sword to get these menaces off the earth"

"Fire!" Valyron shouted inspired by the reason. His voice echoed across the battlefield.

The trebuchet's arm whipped forward, releasing a flaming boulder with terrifying speed. The first shot hit the trees with an explosion of sparks and flames, the crackling fire spreading across the forest floor.

A second boulder was launched, then a third, each one igniting the dark forest, sending flames higher and higher into the sky. The impact shook the ground beneath their feet as the fire consumed everything in its path. The trees screamed as they cracked and splintered, falling like giants to the earth.

Lucifer's eyes never left the forest's edge. He knew the brothers couldn't have gotten too far—every shot from the trebuchet was designed to drive them into the open.

"We're getting closer," he muttered, stepping forward, his hand gripping his sword. "They can't hide from us any longer."

Valyron joined him, not having any choice, his staff gleaming in the firelight. "They may have been hiding, but not for long. They won't be able to outrun the flames."

Leo surveyed the scene. "Do you think this will break them? They've been using the dark forest as their shield. The fire might make them panic."

Lucifer shook his head. "If anything, it'll force them to make a decision. Either they burn with the forest, or they face us directly."

Another volley of boulders struck the trees, and the air grew thick with smoke. The whole forest seemed alive with the sound of cracking wood and the roar of flames. The firelight flickered in Lucifer's eyes, reflecting the resolve that burned within him.

"They can't escape," Lucifer said, his voice colder than ever. "Not tonight."

As the fire spread, the soldiers advanced, forming a perimeter around the burning woods. They would not let the brothers slip away again. They would either show themselves, or the flames would consume everything in their path.

Lucifer felt the heat of the fire against his skin, and he allowed himself a moment of quiet satisfaction. The brothers had underestimated the force of his army. But it wasn't over yet. Not until Elyon and Orin were dealt with.

49

THE SHIELD OF SACRIFICE

The forest crackled with the sounds of war, smoke swirling in the air, the heat of the flames licking at the edges of the trees. The distant clamour of battle echoed all around, but Lucifer's gaze remained locked on Leo and Valyron. Many men had died. He could not afford more, especially his noble warriors. The ones who stood besides him every moments they had been through.

His decision had already been made. A sacrifice was must.

Lucifer had known this moment would come. From the moment they set foot in the forest, he had realized that there was only one way out for them. He could feel it deep within, the pull of the darkness—the energy he had always controlled but now had to release. It was the only way to ensure Leo and Valyron escaped. His body shook with the weight of that knowledge, the finality of it.

Leo looked back at him, his eyes full of doubt. "Lucifer, you can't—"

"I *can*," Lucifer said through gritted teeth, his voice low but firm. "You have to go."

Valyron reached out, but Lucifer held up a hand, his gaze hardening. "Go. I'll hold them off."

"No!" Leo shouted, his voice filled with desperation. "Lucifer, we're not leaving you!"

But Lucifer didn't falter. His body was already drawing on the power he had kept buried for so long—the power of darkness, the very essence that had defined his life. It surged within him, a tempest of energy and anger, and he embraced it fully.

"I said, *go!*" Lucifer roared, his voice commanding and final.

Valyron hesitated for only a heartbeat before Leo pulled him away. They had no choice now. There was no time. But as they turned to leave, a sharp crack pierced the air.

A bullet whistled through the smoke, missing Leo by mere inches, grazing his arm. He cried out, stumbling. The bullet embedded itself in the tree just beside them, splintering the bark with a violent impact.

"Leo!" Valyron shouted, gripping his arm. "We don't have time for this."

Leo clenched his jaw. His arm throbbed, blood seeping through his sleeve, but he knew they couldn't waste another second.

But they couldn't just leave Lucifer.

Leo turned to face his comrade, his heart aching with the decision they were being forced to make. "As a true warrior, I believe in the code," Leo said, his voice firm with resolve, "and what should be done… *Leave no man behind.*"

Lucifer's eyes softened briefly before hardening again. He shook his head, his voice a growl of resignation. "If we do that, Leo… there might be no man left to save."

Leo's gaze flickered for a moment, torn between his duty as a warrior and the reality of their situation. But before he could speak further, a massive shadow fell over them.

Draco landed in front of them, his great wings sending gusts of wind through the trees. His massive form blocked their path, his eyes glowing with an unspoken command. The dragon's powerful presence was undeniable, and yet, there was something almost sorrowful in the way he looked at them.

Leo stopped in his tracks, stunned by the sudden appearance of the creature. "Draco?" he murmured, his voice filled with uncertainty.

The dragon's deep, rumbling voice echoed in the air, low and menacing. "*Go.*" He was not speaking to them; he was commanding them, his voice like thunder as he looked at them with fierce determination. "*You will go now.*"

"Draco…" Leo started, his voice trailing off.

Lucifer's eyes narrowed. "*No more arguing. You know I am stubborn. I can't hold it anymore. This is the only way for us to win. Now go!*"

The urgency in Lucifer's voice hit them like a wave. They could see the finality in his eyes, the weight of what was happening. Lucifer wasn't going to make it, but they still had a chance to survive.

Lucifer stood behind them, his figure silhouetted against the roaring flames as the dark power within him swelled. He didn't look back, his focus entirely on the battle he was about to face. It was too late to save him.

Leo felt his resolve weaken, but with one last look at Lucifer, he knew what had to be done.

Valyron's grip on his arm tightened. "We have to go. Now, Leo."

Leo's heart was heavy as he nodded, but before they could move, Draco stepped forward, his massive body blocking their path once again. His wings spread wide, almost as if he were shielding them from the inevitable fate Lucifer had chosen.

Draco was sad, but he knew what victory meant for Lucifer.

Lucifer's voice broke through the haze of confusion. "*Go, now!*"

Without another word, Leo turned and ran, with Valyron following close behind. They pushed through the thick smoke, their every step weighted with the knowledge that their friend—no, their brother—was facing his end. Draco, with a final, sorrowful glance at Lucifer, turned and followed them as they sprinted toward the clearing.

Valyron, was not ready to leave him behind nor was Leo, but they had no other choice but to leave. Or was there? Valyron thought of a way to save Lucifer. He talked to Leo about it.

"I have a plan to save Lucifer. What if I open a portal and attack from behind. I will cast a spell of shielding on Lucifer and finish what is left of the brothers." Leo was open to all suggestions. He thought it was a great plan. "If there is a chance it works, we must take it. But be safe!" Draco slowed down a little as he understood the new plan. Valyron using his magic, went through the portal. However, there was a distortion caused by the dark forces produced by Lucifer and could not execute the initial plan. Without hesitation he cast a shield on Lucifer but it didn't work as the darkness was so strong, the shield wasn't able to withhold it and deformed.

Lucifer remained behind, a shadow of his former self, his power swirling in the air. The darkness around him grew thicker as he let go of all control. With a final roar, he unleashed everything he had, the full force of his magic crashing against the bullets charging towards him. Trees were ripped from their roots, boulders were thrown like toys, and fire consumed everything in its path. The earth trembled as he let out the power. The brothers managed to shoot one last time.

The chaos of battle raged on, but in that moment, Lucifer knew there was no turning back. He had given everything. As everything was falling apart, he heard a thud.

A bullet flew from the smoke. The brothers had managed to shoot one last time. The sound of it was like the crack of thunder, and it was headed for Lucifer. But in the moment, Valyron jumped in front of him saving Lucifer. he felt it—*that* moment of uncertainty. His heart stopped, just for a beat. He saw Valyron fall in front of him. He had saved Lucifer from a guaranteed death. All that was left was darkness.

Had he failed? Was the noble sacrifice gone in vain?

Before he could dwell on the thought, his vision went black, the darkness within him consuming him entirely.

He had done what was needed to be done.

50

THE LOSS OF THE FALLEN

The battlefield was silent. The air hung heavy with smoke and ash, the forest reduced to charred remnants of its former self. What had once been a place of life now felt like an empty void—a stark reflection of the chaos that had unfolded.

Leo stood alone with Draco. It had been too long. Valyron should have been back by now. The sounds of battle had long since faded, leaving only the hollow whistle of the wind through the scorched trees. Draco stood behind him, his wings beating gently as he surveyed the broken land.

Leo was turning red and grey. He was worried and anxious. He quickly hopped on Draco and told him to fly back to the battlefield. On the way his thoughts were filled with negativity. As he reached, he investigated the entire area. Searching for his friends, in every corner possible. But they were nowhere to be found.

Lucifer was gone.

They had seen him fall. Or so they thought.

Leo's gaze drifted across the wreckage until it landed on a shape lying motionless in the dirt. A body.

His chest tightened. His breath quickened.

No.

"He can't be gone," Leo whispered, his voice strained with desperation. "Lucifer…"

Slowly, he approached the body. His hands trembled as he knelt and pulled back the cloth.

The breath left his lungs in a shattered gasp.

Valyron.

Leo stumbled back, his breath sharp and shallow as Valyron's pale face emerged beneath the fading light. His skin was white as marble, streaked with dirt and blood. His staff lay beside him, splintered down the middle—a jagged reminder of what had been lost.

"No…" Leo's voice was barely a whisper. His knees buckled as he dropped to the ground beside Valyron's still form.

Valyron's chest didn't rise. His lips were slightly parted, his eyes closed as though he was merely sleeping—but the coldness of his skin told a different story.

Leo's hands hovered over Valyron's shoulders. His throat tightened painfully. "This… this isn't happening." His voice cracked. "Valyron, wake up."

Draco lowered his head, his large golden eyes narrowing as he sniffed at Valyron's body. A low, mournful growl rumbled from deep within the dragon's chest, vibrating through the ground beneath Leo's hands.

"No," Leo whispered again, shaking his head as tears blurred his vision. His hands gripped Valyron's tunic, shaking him gently. "You're not gone. You can't be gone."

Draco's wings rustled as the dragon drew back, his gaze fixed toward the distant edge of the battlefield. Leo barely noticed. His eyes were locked on Valyron, searching for any sign of life—anything.

But there was nothing.

He's gone.

The realization cut through him like a blade. His chest constricted painfully, his breath shallow and broken. Valyron had been with him through everything. They had fought side by side, survived impossible odds—and now he was just… gone?

Leo's trembling fingers brushed over Valyron's staff. It was cold beneath his touch. Lifeless. Just like Valyron.

His gaze drifted downward—and then he saw them.

The bloodstains. Dark patches seeping through Valyron's tunic. His breath hitched as he pulled the cloth aside, his stomach twisting violently.

Three bullet holes.

Jagged, dark-edged wounds centred across Valyron's chest. Precise. Lethal.

Leo's hands trembled as he touched the torn fabric. His mind reeled. Bullet wounds. Not magic. Not swords. Something colder. More calculated.

The sharp cracks during the battle—he remembered them now. Gunfire.

Valyron had taken the hits.

For them.

Leo's jaw clenched as his eyes squeezed shut. A burning knot of grief twisted deep inside his chest. Valyron had always fought for them. He had always shielded them. And now…

Now it had cost him everything.

A cold breeze swept through the clearing, stirring the ash beneath Leo's knees. The ground was littered with shattered weapons and broken bodies. A ruinous silence hung over it all.

Valyron had been with them. Lucifer must have seen Valyron fall. And then…

Leo's fists curled at his sides. He could imagine the look in Lucifer's eyes—shock, grief… and something darker. Lucifer had stood over Valyron's body, his hands shaking as he covered him with the cloth. And then… he left.

Why?

Draco let out a low huff, his golden eyes narrowing toward the distant tree line. His tail swept across the ground, scattering ash.

Leo's gaze sharpened. If Lucifer had survived… why hadn't he come back? Why leave Valyron like this?

A sound broke through the silence—a faint, rhythmic crunch of footsteps over loose earth.

Leo's breath hitched.

Draco's head lifted sharply, looking towards the smoke-filled horizon. His wings spread slightly, casting a shadow over Leo as his growl deepened.

Leo rose to his feet, his hand drifting to the dagger at his side. His pulse hammered in his ears as the footsteps grew louder.

No figure emerged from the smoke.

The steps stopped.

Silence.

Leo's breath hitched. His gaze darted toward Valyron's still form. His chest tightened painfully.

"I'm going to find him," Leo whispered, his voice low and sharp.

Draco lowered his head beside Leo, his golden gaze steady.

Leo's jaw set, his hands curling into fists at his sides. His grief burned beneath his skin, but beneath it, anger stirred—a quiet, dangerous heat.

Lucifer had left. And Leo was going to find him: dead or alive.

www.ingramcontent.com/pod-product-compliance
Lightning Source LLC
LaVergne TN
LVHW041709070526
838199LV00045B/1272